THE GIFT OF ACABAR

*The touching story of a boy who does indeed
capture a star—and learns from that star
that heavenly secrets are to be found
right here on earth.*

"What a beautiful story Og and Buddy have
written. It reminds us again of the things that
are hidden deep in our hearts that we occasion-
ally see but keep forgetting."
—Jesse Lair,
author of *I Ain't Much Baby
But I'm All I've Got*

"A life must change from within, and this book
is the prescription for such change."
—N. Eldon Tanner
President, The Church of Jesus
Christ of Latter-Day Saints

The Gift of Acabar

OG MANDINO *and* BUDDY KAYE

BANTAM BOOKS
TORONTO · NEW YORK · LONDON · SYDNEY

THE GIFT OF ACABAR
A Bantam Book

PRINTING HISTORY
Lippincott edition published September 1978
A selection of the Christian Herald Family Bookshelf,
December 1978.

A condensation appeared in Success Unlimited Magazine,
June 1979.

Bantam edition / August 1979
2nd printing

Bantam Books are published by Bantam Books, Inc. Its trade-
mark, consisting of the words "Bantam Books" and the por-
trayal of a bantam, is Registered in U.S. Patent and Trademark
Office and in other countries. Marca Registrada. Bantam
Books, Inc., 666 Fifth Avenue, New York, New York 10019.

PRINTED IN THE UNITED STATES OF AMERICA

FOR THOSE WHO
STILL BELIEVE IN MIRACLES

Everyone's life is a fairy tale,
    written by God's fingers.
—HANS CHRISTIAN ANDERSEN

The Gift
of
Acabar

Prologue

☆

They were wandering and hunting across more than one hundred thousand square miles of primeval wilderness, now called Lapland, long before Romulus and Remus founded Rome and Homer wrote the *Iliad*, long before the Hebrews entered Canaan and Stonehenge was erected in Britain, long before the Tassili rock paintings were scratched on the caves of Algeria and the great pyramid for Khufu was completed, long before Nebuchadnezzar built his hanging gardens and Gautama Buddha preached in India. The world knows them as Lapps but they call themselves Same, and there are no more than thirty-five thousand scattered in isolated villages and cabins throughout the northernmost regions of Norway, Sweden, Finland, and even Russia.

They have suffered the most vicious of climates with courage and patience. They have tended to their families with love and compassion and trained their young, by example, in the art of living and self-reliance . . . and they have endured. They have never had a country or even a state they could call

1

their own, nor have they ever accepted aid from any government.

They are small in stature yet big of heart. No stranger is ever turned away from their doors nor are their homes ever locked. Crime and divorce are virtually unknown except for what they read in their few newspapers or hear on their radios.

The Lapp people have been a credit to the race of man for more than eight thousand years, yet less is known about them than about any other people on the face of this planet. Certainly, in the mysterious cycles of eternity, their moment in the spotlight of history was long overdue.

And so it came to pass that once upon a time . . . but not very long ago, mind you . . . in a small and desolate Lapland village far north of the Arctic Circle . . . a miracle occurred.

If only the world had known. . . .

One

☆

The plaintive cry of a solitary wolf echoed in the outside blackness, the dreaded sound penetrating the walls of every home and cabin in Kalvala as it swept through the desolate village on the first angry winds of winter.

Tulo Mattis dropped his pencil and pushed aside the green leather-covered ledger. He held his breath and listened. The wolf howled again until a single rifle shot crackled across the frozen tundra.

With a sigh of relief Tulo rose from the table and limped painfully toward his sister's small bedroom. He paused to stroke Nikku's thick gray fur as he passed the slumbering spitz.

"Dog, you are getting old and lazy. I can remember when a howling wolf would have had you tearing holes in the door."

As he approached Jaana's bed her frightened voice came from beneath many blankets. "Tulo, did you hear that wolf?"

"Yes. Uncle Varno must have shot him. No harm will ever come to our reindeer while he stands

3

guard. And no harm will come to you either, so go to sleep, little girl."

The green ledger was still open when he returned to the kitchen table. Tulo pulled it toward him until it was directly under the unshaded light bulb and read the words he had written to mark his fourteenth birthday:

December 12

The dark time is now upon us.
It is two months to sunrise.
But even if the summer's midnight sun were shining and the heather and goldenrod still covered our meadow this would be the saddest birthday of my life. What my sister and I have lost in the past twelve months can never be recovered.
I have read that one can always find a seed of happiness in every adversity if one looks for it. I have searched in vain, and all I have for my effort is a pain in my heart that will not go away.
I must not lose hope. I must remain strong for Jaana's sake.

Tulo slowly closed the ledger. He brushed the moisture from his large brown eyes, turned toward the small oval gold-framed photograph which was always on the table, and cupped his mother's image in both hands. In the sounds of the wind he was certain he could hear her warm voice once again.

"My son, God must have special plans for you. How else can one explain your gift with words? Someday your name will be honored by all our people, and the words you write will be bound in leather so that their truth and beauty can endure and light the entire world like a star of hope."

Sobs shook Tulo's small body. He raised the

photograph to his lips and kissed the glass, again and again. "Mama . . . Mama . . . I miss you . . . I miss you . . . I miss you. . . ."

Nikku's impatient scratching against the door interrupted Tulo's self-pity. Out of habit he pulled on his woolen cloak and the four-pointed cap that Jaana had knit and followed the dog on his nightly trek to the meadow.

The snow had ceased, the clouds had passed, and now the wind was only a soft whisper. Above, instead of its usual star-flecked dark-blue pigment, the sky was a rippling patchwork of luminescent colors. Flames of sun-bright intensity leaped upward, cascading billows of sparkling green particles against soaring eruptions of lavender and gold. The boy had never seen the northern lights perform so brilliantly. Even the snow under his feet rippled from the shimmering aurora, transforming the meadow into a magic lake filled with rubies and emeralds and opals and diamonds.

Tulo was so captivated by the dancing lights that he forgot to be sad. He even forgot his injured knee as he skipped and danced through vagrant snowdrifts, laughing and singing and scooping large chunks of white crystals which sparkled like diamond dust when he showered them on Nikku. Finally he reached the big tree, where he fell gasping for breath while his snow-drenched animal crouched close by, barking impatiently for their romp to begin again. Instead, Tulo lay back and watched the tumbling coronas of heavenly fire continue to change color between the thick silhouette of pine boughs.

The big tree had been a village landmark longer

than the oldest resident could remember. Its sturdy trunk reached more than fifteen meters into the sky in a land where dark and interminable sub-zero winters and brief summers produced only dwarf willows, scraggly birches, stunted spruce and pine. The tree's needles were long and green, and its branches constantly multiplied and grew as if its roots were being nourished in a lush tropical forest. Some said it had been planted, centuries ago, by Stallo, the legendary giant of the Same people, and one side of its trunk, close to the ground, had been rubbed free of bark by those who believed that contact with its wood was enough to bring good fortune. Jaana called it her star tree, innocently insisting that stars, at least from her low vantage point, actually hung like fruit from its massive limbs. No one disputed her.

The big tree, above all, had become a symbol of hope to both young and old of Kalvala, a living example that it was possible not only to survive but also to grow tall and flourish, even under the worst of conditions.

Tulo suddenly sat up and rested his back against the rough bark. A strange thought had occurred to him as the northern lights continued to swirl in iridescent patterns across the sky. "Old dog, do you suppose those wise men of our ancestors, those shamans who once protected our people with their drums and magic words, do you suppose they spoke the truth when they said that if one whistled at the northern lights one could call the dead?"

Nikku barked, ready for more play with his young master.

"I wonder. I wonder."

6

Softly, Tulo began to whistle the tune to a lullaby that his mother had often sung to Jaana when she was still in her wooden cradle. He shaped his small hands into a horn and aimed shrill notes up toward the brightest pennant of flashing color.

Then he closed his eyes . . . and as the lullaby's melancholy melody continued to float skyward through the fluttering pine needles, his thoughts moved backward through time to events of his brief past that had already shaped his life and would eventually seal his destiny in a way Tulo could never foresee as he sat under the star tree . . . and whistled at heaven.

Two

☆

Pedar Mattis had carved a small pair of skis for his son soon after the child took his first stumbling steps. Like all other Lapp children, Tulo mastered the small wooden runners quickly and before he was three years old he could ski all the way to LaVeeg's village store and return without assistance.

By his fifth birthday Tulo could handle a lasso well enough to rope any reluctant reindeer. Pedar also taught him how to fish through ice, how to use and care for his knife, how to cure a reindeer hide, how to chew sinew into twine, and how to raise their summer tent. Later Pedar schooled him in the art of controlling a flat-bottomed sledge and in the techniques for tracking their hated enemy, the wolf, including the use of his ski pole to defend himself and their reindeer against any attacker.

For Pedar and Inga Mattis, who still held to the proud customs of the Same people, the reindeer was the most important element in their lives. Standing no more than four feet tall and weighing less than

8

three hundred pounds when fully grown, this amazing but timid creature could endure a climate that would kill most domesticated animals. The Mattis herd, numbering nearly two hundred, provided milk, meat, clothing, and even money when some were sold at the annual fall roundup. Nothing of the reindeer was ever wasted. Its tongue was used for stew, the blood was dried for the dogs, the bone marrow was a delicacy for teething children, and the horns were carved into knife handles and art objects.

The years passed swiftly, and the fortune of the Mattis family was exceedingly good. Each summer they migrated with their animals to the bountiful green foothills several days' journey from Kalvala, and while they camped on the mountain slopes, warmed by the midnight sun, the reindeer does brought forth many calves. Both their herd and their happy memories multiplied with the passing seasons.

Tulo's fondest recollections, however, were not of those sun-drenched days and nights on the mountains but of the dark days and nights of winter when the sun disappeared for more than two months and father and son watched over their reindeer in the rolling hills, called fells, near their village cabin in Kalvala.

Burrowed deeply into the snow to escape the savage winds and freezing cold, father and son would sit close to their small fire and brew hot coffee. Then Pedar would watch with undisguised amusement as the lad tried to emulate him by holding a lump of sugar between his teeth while drinking the scalding liquid. As with everything else

Tulo attempted, he soon mastered this difficult Same custom.

One quiet night, while the reindeer endlessly foraged and pawed through the snow in search of their favorite moss, Tulo lay close to his father with his head resting on Pedar's thigh. After staring up at the heavens for several moments he asked, "Papa, how many stars are there?"

"I do not know, son. Millions, I imagine."

"Are they very far away?"

"They are so far away that if the swiftest buzzard flew directly at one, from here, he could not reach it in his lifetime."

"How big are the stars?"

"Your grandfather, who was very wise, once told me that while our sun is more than one hundred times larger than this earth it is considered only a small star compared to the size of some you see up there."

"Papa, why does our sun go away and leave us in darkness for so many weeks, every winter, and then return and shine on us, day and night, in the summer?"

Pedar shook his head helplessly. "Tulo, you must remember that there were no schools here when I was your age. I am not sure how to answer you, but I believe it has something to do with how our world tilts toward the sun and then away from it at different times of the year and how we are located near the top." He reached down and tenderly ran his fingers across the child's face. "Your mama says that the months of darkness and cold we endure are a small price to pay for living on the roof of the world, so close to God."

"Yes, I know. Papa, if the sun went away one winter but did not return in the spring, what would happen to us?"

Pedar slowly tamped tobacco into his pipe and wasted several matches before it was lit. As he exhaled a long curl of pungent smoke he replied, "If the sun did not return I'm afraid we would soon perish."

"Why?"

"Because no plants could grow in the darkness, and if there were no grass and willow and moss our reindeer would starve. Without them we would have no food or clothing or money, and life would be impossible here for any reindeer family."

Tulo pondered his father's words and then asked, "Could God stop the sun from coming back to us in the spring if He wanted to?"

"God can do everything, my son."

After another brief silence: "Papa, I just saw a star fly across the sky and then disappear. Are those very small stars that do that?"

"Yes, I believe so."

"If they are small do they ever land here so that we can see how they look and maybe even touch them?"

Pedar sighed. "I do not know, Tulo."

"Papa, I would like to know more about the stars . . . the sun . . . and God . . . and everything."

On the following morning, while their son was still in bed, Pedar leaned across the table and grasped both his wife's hands. Puzzled by her husband's unusual silence during breakfast, Inga tilted her head and waited.

"Inga, I don't know whether it is because his

11

mind is so bright or I am so stupid, but already Tulo is asking questions of me that I am unable to answer. I realize he is not scheduled to begin school until next fall but I do not think we should wait. Let us enroll him now."

"If that is your wish, Pedar. But you two have been very close. The separation will not be easy for either of you."

"What must be, must be. Our world here is changing. Our grazing lands are growing smaller and smaller, and our people can move no farther north or we shall be in cold waters. The tourists are coming with the new highway. The factories and mining people and power plants are already near. Now we have electricity instead of oil for our lamps, and airplanes fly over our herds. Yesterday I heard talk of something called a snowmobile that can travel over the snow faster than any reindeer or man on skis. Tulo must be educated as soon as possible to cope with a new way of life he cannot avoid."

"And you?"

"Me, I shall never change. I'll be a reindeer man until I die."

"But not a lonely one."

"What do you mean?"

Inga rose and began stacking the dishes. Then she leaned over her frowning husband, seized his nose between her thumb and forefinger, and gently squeezed. "I mean, Mr. Professor, that soon you will have another small pupil to follow you around while Tulo is in school."

Three

⭐

Arrol Nobis, Kalvala's young schoolmaster, was almost a foot taller than most Lapps, who rarely exceed five feet in height. He stretched his tall, thin frame before the fireplace while both Pedar and Inga remained politely silent.

"I have come to talk with you both about Tulo."

Pedar removed his pipe from his mouth and held it poised in midair. "He has been causing you trouble?"

"Oh, no. He is well-mannered and polite and there is no problem with discipline. It is his mind that—"

"His mind?" Pedar interrupted. "What is wrong with his mind?"

"Nothing is wrong with it, Pedar. At the university we were taught never to despair of a student so long as he has even one clear idea. Tulo has bushels of clear ideas! Never before have I had a student who so far surpassed his classmates as your son. With Tulo, to read a lesson once is sufficient. And his questions! He is always seeking an

13

explanation to everything. Why? . . . Why? . . . Why? That is his favorite word. Already he has devoured every book in our small library. Now he is reading them again. He has even read the Bible three times! I have never known a child such as yours."

Pedar glanced at Inga and nodded, pleased that the schoolmaster's opinion confirmed his own judgment about Tulo's early enrollment.

By now Arrol was pacing back and forth and waving his arms. "That is not all. Since he is already proficient in reading and writing Same, he now wants me to teach him Finnish and Swedish. Pedar, those are not part of a student's selective curriculum until the age of ten. But Tulo tells me, and unfortunately he is correct, that there are not enough books printed in Same for him to learn all the things he wants to know. I tell you, he is so . . . so different! Most of the children attend school only because they must. They would much rather be skiing or fishing or hunting. Not Tulo! And his stories and poems—"

Inga broke her silence. "Stories? Poems?"

"Your son is writing poems and stories that are far superior to any ever before produced in my school. And he has a mind that can create a fantasy out of the most simple act of nature. His compositions—beautifully constructed, I might add—make our legends and folk tales seem dull by comparison. If he continues on the course he now pursues he will someday be a fine writer . . . a rarity among our people."

Pedar, no longer feeling self-satisfied, shook his

14

head in bewilderment. "What should we do, Arrol?"

"There is only one thing to do, my friends. Water the plant. Fertilize it. Protect it and love it and help it all you can so that it can grow to its fullest potential."

"How? You know us. We have only a small herd and little education, Inga and I."

"Books, Pedar, books! Great minds need books on which to feed as much as the reindeer need the moss to survive our winters. Give him books ... and more books. If you wish I'll review the catalogs our school receives from the publishers in Rovaniemi and Helsinki. I'll make a list of volumes that I would recommend, and if you are willing to purchase them for Tulo I'll order them. Then he can read and learn at his own pace. He is something very special, your son. . . . Oh, I almost forgot. There is one more thing."

"More?" Pedar laughed nervously. "You have just told us that our son is a wonder child. There is more?"

Arrol smiled for the first time and patted his friend's shoulder sympathetically. "Pedar, have you ever flown kites?"

"Kites? Kites? When would I have ever found time to fly kites? I have never even seen a kite in all my life."

"Well, my friend, you will soon see plenty of them."

Pedar turned to Inga and motioned toward the fireplace. "I think our schoolmaster should have another cup of hot coffee to help him recover his senses. I'm afraid the strain of managing forty

15

children has finally affected his mind—and there are still two months before his vacation."

"Pedar, listen to me! Tulo found an old book, translated from English by a seventeenth-century missionary, dealing with the history of kites and how to build and fly them. He has become completely captivated by the idea of flying his own. Right now, as I talk to you, he is back there at school building a kite according to the specifications he found in the book. Among other things he has now become an expert on kites. He can tell you all about the first kites flown in China; he can explain how the giant kites of Japan, many weighing more than a ton, are raised from the ground; and he knows all about the kite flown by the American, Benjamin Franklin, when he experimented with lightning. Kites, Pedar, kites!"

"You are telling us that we have produced a son who wants to write stories and poems and fly kites instead of herding reindeer?"

"Yes."

The young father rose and emptied his pipe into the flames, noisily tapping it against the fireplace bricks. He stared at the crackling logs while Inga and Arrol watched in silence. Finally he shrugged his shoulders. "Very well. Let us begin to water this amazing plant that has sprung up in our poor garden. Arrol, please order whatever you believe he should read, and I shall gladly pay you."

"Thank you, Pedar."

"No, no, dear friend, it is Inga and I who thank you—with all our hearts—for the loving interest you have shown in our son. How fortunate we are to have you."

"Pedar, the opportunity and challenge to work with a gifted child rarely ever comes to a teacher. God has placed that boy in our trust for some unknown purpose. We must not fail either Tulo . . . or God."

Long after the schoolmaster was gone the young couple still pondered the meaning of his parting words.

When spring returned and the reindeer moved north, Inga was once again in the lead sledge, with her husband skiing ahead and her infant daughter, Jaana, safely cradled between her knees.

Tulo's sledge, following that of his mother, was filled with boxes of books. All summer long, whenever his chores allowed, he read and studied and wrote, and when his nose was not between the pages of a book or pad he could be found on the rocky slopes holding tightly to a thick willow branch wrapped with twine.

The twine would sing in the clear air as it reached up and up . . . and at its end flew a small red kite. As Tulo watched his kite twist and turn in the blazing sun it was a simple matter for him to transform that soaring diamond of scarlet into a warlike dragon or a giant butterfly, even a lazy swan, until finally it would be caught in a treacherous downdraft, plummet toward the ground like an attacking eagle . . . and crash!

With an agonizing cry its proud creator always raced across the fields to retrieve his fallen angel. He would press it to his thin bosom and speak comforting words to it. Then he would carry it gently back to the family tent to mend its wounds.

Tomorrow it would fly again.

Four

☆

A worried Inga moved closer to her husband as the first group of frightened reindeer were being driven into the center corral. She tugged at Pedar's cloak and then whispered so that Tulo, standing only a few paces away, could not hear, "Is he ready for this?"

For four years there had been joy and contentment in the Mattis family, and each year always reached its climax in the festive autumnal roundup in which they and every other reindeer family participated.

Pedar turned to watch Tulo make practice throws with his lasso. He nodded confidently. "He is almost thirteen. I was much younger when I worked my first roundup."

"Yes, but the reindeer were your whole life when you were a boy. Our son has spent far more time with his books and his writing than he has with the animals."

"That is true, and he can handle a kite line much better than the lasso. Still, I have no heart to refuse his help. He would be brokenhearted if we caused him to lose face with the other boys who are ~~~ ing with their fathers."

"Have you heard what some of them are calling him?"

"No."

"Kite boy! They are calling our son 'kite boy'! Even Varno's oldest, Erkki, asked him if there was a tail on his lasso, and Raimo's two boys wondered if he expected to catch reindeer with a bookmark instead of his rope. I don't like it, Pedar."

"And what did Tulo say?"

"Nothing. He just smiled and turned away."

Pedar's jaws tightened. "Well, we'll show them. Are you ready? I see some of our animals in this group."

During the carefree summer days their reindeer had roamed at will, grazing and intermingling freely with reindeer from other village herds. Now, following the roundup of every animal on the mountain slopes, each family had to separate its own reindeer from the others before the long journey back to Kalvala for the winter. Inga hastened toward the small fenced enclosure which had been assigned to them and waited.

Pedar and Tulo climbed the splintered fencing and leaped down onto the dusty floor of the main corral. Standing close to the boards they watched and waited as the frightened animals thundered past, antlers slashing wildly, sharp hooves spewing sand and pebbles in every direction. Suddenly Pedar yelled, "There's one of ours. Take him, son!"

Tulo spotted their family's identifying ear nick on a large stag. Calmly he twirled his lasso over his head as the snorting animal charged closer. He s wrist and the rope whistled through the pping gently around the bobbing head. The tugged and bucked, almost pulling Tulo from his feet before ceasing its struggle and placidly walking toward its captor, who was exultantly reeling in his rope. Pedar pounded his son's shoulders proudly, and Tulo acknowledged the compliment with a wink. Then he led his catch toward the family corral while Inga unlatched their gate.

"That was perfect, son!" she shouted.

"Thank you, Mama. I'll be back with many more."

The lassoing and separation continued throughout the day, and father and son worked steadily with only a brief pause for food. Whenever they roped one of their does her new calf would follow, and Pedar would hold it gently while Tulo punched their mark on the bewildered infant's left ear. Then the youth always stroked the long-legged calf before leading it gently to their corral.

The final group of animals was driven into the arena just as the sun began to set. Smoke from many family bonfires mixed with the flying sand from the corral and billowed in heavy clouds over the raucous bedlam of men and animals as lassos incessantly cut into the herd from all sides. The herders were in a hurry to claim the remainder of their reindeer ahead of the fast-falling darkness.

A weary Pedar nudged his son. "There's our big monster with the broken antler. I'll take that one!"

"Please, Papa!" Tulo pleaded. "Let me handle him. All day long you've given me only the easy ones to rope. Watch me! I'll show you! I'm as good as any of the other children. Watch!"

Pedar stepped back reluctantly but with a tight smile of admiration creasing his lower cheeks. He nodded. His young son gripped the rope and waited. Soon Tulo once again spotted the shattered horn through the dust. Head bobbing, eyes distended, the bulky animal approached and veered toward the fence. Tulo stepped back calmly, like the most expert of matadors, flipped the rope skyward, and watched it settle softly over the snorting head. Just as Tulo pulled on the lasso a terrified calf, bawling for its misplaced mother, raced between his legs. Off balance, Tulo was jerked from his feet by the rope tied to his left wrist. The lassoed beast swerved and bucked, dragging the boy along the churned surface into the path of the charging herd.

Tulo heard his father's anguished scream. Then he felt sharp pains in his arms as the sleeves of his woolen shirt were ripped away by the gravel. His small frame began to bob and jerk as the desperate animal tossed his head wildly to be free of the rope.

Pedar was already racing toward his son when he saw the rope snap. Instantly he leaped forward, landing on Tulo's blood-streaked back, covering his son's small body with his own. Scores of rockhard hooves immediately pounded over both of them.

On the following morning Uncle Varno carried Tulo's bruised body to his sledge, taking care that his nephew's right leg and its makeshift splint were cushioned by several blankets. He handed the single leather rein to Tulo and passed the harness back to the second sledge where Inga sat, head bowed, with Jaana in front of her. Finally Varno attached the rein to the last two sledges and slapped the lead reindeer lightly.

Tulo sat motionless, the strap wrapped loosely around his right hand. Tears ran down his cheeks but he ignored them. He turned in his sledge, as far as his splinted limb would allow, and nodded to his mother, who stared back. Jaana waved excitedly and called his name, over and over, unaware in her childish innocence that behind her, in the third sledge, was the carefully wrapped body of her father being borne back to Kalvala for burial.

Five

When Tulo opened his eyes he could see his mother tenderly applying oil to his leg, although he could not feel her hands. With her head lowered, Inga did not realize that her son was awake as she massaged his discolored knee, a treatment that had been repeated twice a day since Dr. Malni, from the clinic, had removed the cast just before Christmas.

In her soft voice Inga was speaking aloud. "Dear God, he is so small and you are so big. He is so frail and you are so powerful. Do not abandon him now, God. Let him walk again . . . please."

Tulo felt something cool touch his knee . . . and then again . . . and again. Mama was crying. Her tears fell like drops from a melting spring icicle on his twisted limb.

"Mama, I can feel you! I feel your tears! I feel your hands now! Please don't cry!"

The basin of oil splashed to the floor. Inga covered her pale cheeks with both hands and screamed, "Truly, Tulo, truly? Oh, thank God!"

"Yes! And look, I can wiggle my toes a little!"

Inga knelt and kissed the injured knee. "Soon you will be walking and running as good as ever. I told you! I told you!"

Later, when she brought him food, there was a strange expression on Tulo's face. After she had placed the tray between his knees she asked, "What's the matter, son?"

"Mama, when you ask God for help do you believe he hears you?"

"Of course. He hears everyone, whether they speak the words aloud or in their hearts."

"Does he ever answer you?"

"Always. Look what has happened here today."

"He *always* does what you ask of him?"

"Oh . . . no."

Tulo was perplexed. "Then he doesn't always answer you?"

Inga smiled and her eyes widened. "Oh, I always receive an answer. But since God's plans are not known to any of us, sometimes his answer is no."

In the trying days that followed, Tulo attempted to walk on the injured leg every day, and each time it buckled he would fall back on his bed despondently. Still, Inga would not allow her son to pity himself. If he persisted he would succeed, she assured him. Tomorrow would be better. Soon God, who was very busy, would answer their prayers. They had only to wait . . . to keep trying . . . and believe.

While he waited, Tulo had four visitors. The first was Pastor Bjork, a plump man with white hair and gold spectacles who had officiated at the marriage of Inga and Pedar fifteen years earlier. Erno Bjork's small church was always in a state of

24

physical disrepair, but he maintained that the little money he received from his parishioners was better spent in helping those in need rather than on such unimportant things as paint and nails. He once said, in a sermon, that whenever one saw a large and pretentious church one could be certain that it was a monument to the pastor's vanity rather than an altar for God.

Pastor Bjork brought Tulo a book, *The History of the Same People*, and Tulo read it in three days, fascinated and amazed to learn that more than eighteen centuries ago the Roman historian Tacitus had written about the wild Fenni tribes, Tulo's ancestors; and Ottar, a Norwegian explorer, in the year 892 called the Same people "hunters who also keep reindeer."

For the first time since his accident Tulo wanted to write. He even began a poem about the proud legacy of the Same people. Pastor Bjork's wisely chosen gift had been more beneficial than any platitudes.

Tulo's next two visitors, days later, were Uncle Varno and his son, Erkki. Although her brother-in-law had come to Inga almost on a daily basis, to offer his assistance in any way he could, this was the first meeting between Erkki and Tulo since his cousin had chided him at the corral about not having a kite's tail on his lasso.

Varno and Inga watched anxiously from the bedroom doorway as an embarrassed Erkki approached Tulo's bed and mumbled, "I hope you will be walking soon, cousin Tulo." The older boy clumsily dropped a brown-paper-wrapped package close to Tulo's injured knee and stepped back. Tulo impatiently tore off the covering to reveal a large green leather-bound ledger.

"It is a diary," Erkki explained, "and in it you can write what happens to you each day. There are more than one thousand pages in it, if you count both sides!"

Tulo thumbed through the lined pages and thanked Erkki, unwilling to hurt Uncle Varno's feelings by telling them both that it was not a diary but a bookkeeper's ledger of some sort. When they were gone and he explained his gift to Inga, there was laughter in the Mattis home for the first time since their return to Kalvala. Inga held her sides and howled with glee when Tulo dryly remarked, "With all our money, Mama, this will certainly come in handy."

As spring gradually returned to the land, Tulo's frustration increased. Despite his own persistent efforts and his mother's encouragement he was unable to stand and walk even one step without falling, yet he stubbornly refused the use of an old cane that Inga had discovered in their attic. Canes were for old people, he declared.

Arrol Nobis, the young schoolmaster, was the fourth visitor. A newspaper was under his arm when Inga greeted him, but unlike the others he declined her invitation to enter her son's bedroom. Instead, he positioned himself outside the invalid's room and motioned for Inga to pull back the reindeer skin covering the doorway so that Tulo could see him.

Arrol spread open the front page of the newspaper and held it up with both hands. "Tulo Mattis," he intoned, "do you know what this is?"

26

"It is a newspaper," came the hesitant response from the bedroom.

"And what is its name?"

"*Sabmelas.*"

"That is correct. This is the latest issue. Now, you cannot see it from there but it has a very fine article in these two columns at the right of this front page."

Silence.

"It was written by a very talented individual."

Silence.

"You, especially, would appreciate this writer's style and his way with words. It is a marvelous article on man's love affair with kites." The schoolmaster paused and smiled. "I took the liberty of submitting this piece without the author's permission."

Inga stared at the schoolmaster, the meaning of his words now clear to her. Wide-eyed, she turned her head just as Tulo emerged from his bedroom and shuffled uncertainly across the room, arms outstretched for balance. When he was close he clutched the schoolmaster's chest with both hands for support.

Bracing his favorite pupil with one arm, Arrol Nobis bowed gallantly toward Inga and with a half-sweeping motion toward her son said, "Dear lady, I would like you to meet our very own Lazarus."

That night, believing that his life had indeed been restored, Tulo made his first entry in the green ledger that became his trusted diary.

Six

☆

Memories.

They are like the stars, always with us night and day, waiting patiently for their next appearance.

As he sat under the star tree and whistled to the northern lights, Tulo had been able to recall, vividly, the earlier milestones of his young life. But even their celestial powers failed when he tried to remember, in some logical sequence, all that had happened since that day, almost a year ago, when he had limped haltingly across the floor to Arrol Nobis and proudly read his first published work. Just as merciful unconsciousness often clouds great pain from our senses, Tulo's mind had almost succeeded in blocking out the painful events of the past nine months.

The green ledger! Of course. Ever since cousin Erkki had given him that ponderous leather-bound volume with its tinted lined pages, held fast by three steel pins, he had made daily entries in it as faithfully as the most conscientious bookkeeper.

It was all there, and for reasons he could not understand he wanted to relive it again, now!

Tulo hurried back to the cabin. Beginning with the first ledger page he paused only at specific dates that led him, without sympathy, to the present.

March 16

This was a happy day. Dr. Malni came to check my knee and told Mama that he did not believe we would have to sell our herd in order to pay for specialists at the hospital in Inari. He expects that soon I will be able to walk with only a little limp. When he was gone Mama knelt down and thanked God. I did too.

March 25

Mama teased me when she saw me writing in the ledger this morning. She said that when she had predicted that someday my words would be bound in leather for all the world to share she had more than a bookkeeping ledger in mind. I guess even Mr. Nobis is disappointed that my article in the newspaper has not inspired me to write very much. Someday soon I'll surprise them both.

April 2

Mama was gone for many hours again. She is up to something, for every time she returns she carries another covered box up to the attic, where Jaana and I are now forbidden to go. Whenever I ask her what she is doing she just smiles and changes the subject.

April 7

Mr. Nobis sent me a book filled with wise sayings. On page 9 he had circled one, by Seneca, in red crayon. It said, "There is nothing in the world so much admired as a man who knows how to bear unhappiness

29

with courage." I wish I could talk with Seneca but I know he's been dead for a long, long time.

April 11

The village held their annual reindeer races today. I'm almost glad that Papa was not here to see me make a fool of myself. With Reino pulling I was leading in the first heat until we reached the halfway boulder. As we turned to race for the finish line my bad knee gave way and Reino galloped to the finish line without me. I still have not told Mama but I have put my skis away.

April 14

I'm writing this as I sit under our star tree in the meadow. I know our tree is supposed to have magic power to help anyone who seeks to change his fortune, but so far, even though I rub its bark often, nothing seems to happen. Mama says the tree's magic will only work for those who are ready to help themselves.

April 18

Uncle Varno and Mama have been having many talks together. Now I know why. Uncle is going to take our herd, along with his, to the mountains this summer, and Mama will pay him for his trouble with one third of all the new calves that our animals foal. She did not tell me her reasons but I'm certain she feels that on the slopes she cannot take care of a young daughter, a herd of reindeer, and a son who would be very little help to her. I miss Papa very much today.

April 23

This morning I ran to the star tree and back to the house. Tomorrow I shall do it twice and the next day three times. Soon my leg will be as strong as before the accident. Mama does so much for us that I cannot let her down. I want to be able to help her as Papa used to do. If I am the man of the family, as Mama says, it is about time I began acting like one.

The terrible mosquitoes have come, and today all the reindeer began to move north. Uncle Varno left us old Kala, for transportation, and three animals for meat, but he took all our dogs except Nikku. Mama cried when everyone rode away. We all cried. It is the first time in our lives we have not gone to the mountains with our herd for the summer.

May 19

I found my old kite in the shed and brought it to the meadow. It flies as well as ever, and it was fun to let the twine roll from the wooden reel that Papa made and watch that pretty red thing fly so high I could barely see it. I wonder how high a kite has ever flown? My knee pains me now but it was good to find something I can still do well.

May 27

We have moved for the summer. The tent that we always used on the mountain slopes has now been raised next to the great highway about twelve kilometers from Kalvala. It seems that those boxes Mama has been collecting are filled with handicrafts made by the people of our village, and now she has arranged them on shelves along the roadside to sell to tourists.

We have rows of carved horn spoons, belts, moccasins, reindeer hats, and hundreds of tiny wooden animals, and Mama keeps a strict record of every piece she sells. When we go back to the village, in the fall, she will return the unsold goods along with half the price she receives on those she sells.

Mama said that if we all work hard we might be able to save enough so that I can still enroll at the university in two years. Perhaps all my wishing under the star tree has not been in vain.

June 6

Our new business is doing very well. A truckload of fishermen, on the way to the Varanger Peninsula,

31

stopped and asked for coffee today. Mama quickly brewed a pot, and now we also sell coffee. Later, a tourist bus stopped and some of the passengers asked if we would pose for a picture in front of our tent. Mama charged them each five markkas. She keeps telling us that we can make any dream come true if we work hard, ask for God's help, and never give up.

July 13

Mama has been coughing for the last few days. I think she is working too hard. Since we have twenty-four hours of sunlight the traffic continues at all hours, and Mama sleeps very little for fear she might lose a sale. Jaana and I really try to help her, but Mama wants to wait on every customer herself. She was so tired tonight that she let Jaana cook for us. Jaana will make a good wife for someone when she grows up.

July 29

Business is very good but Mama is ill. She has grown very thin and her color is strange, almost gray. She is coughing more than ever but she doesn't pay attention to me when I ask her to rest. I'm frightened. There is no one closer to us than the village in case something should happen to her. It is not easy to be the man of the family.

September 30

Mama is dead. I could not make myself write those words until today. She died on the night of the second of August while she slept. Earlier that evening, for the first time, she asked Jaana and me to take care of customers while she took a nap. A little later I heard her calling my name and ran to the tent. She reached out and took my hand and held it over her heart. Then she pulled me close and kissed me and said, "Tulo, I love you. Take care of your sister but remember that your destiny is beyond Kalvala. Look up. Reach out. God and the star tree will help you." Then she slept. When we awoke the next morning Mama was dead.

I do not remember anything about the funeral excep.
that they buried Mama next to Papa in the cemetery.
Uncle Varno and Aunt Stina have asked us to come
live with them, but Jaana and I have decided to remain
in our own cabin and take care of each other.

Tulo wearily pushed aside the green ledger. He had, indeed, whistled to the northern lights and, at least in his mind, recalled the past . . . and the dead. But what of tomorrow? he wondered. And the next day? What would the future bring for his small sister and him?

He rose, went to the front door, and opened it to blackness. Masses of low dark clouds from the west blotted out every vestige of the heavenly lights. The wind screamed fiercely now across the tundra, and the snow was falling once again.

A little boy lost softly caressed the small photograph of his mother once more and limped off to bed.

Seven

☆

The northern lights had once again served as the dreaded omen of bad weather, and the blizzard that now ravaged Kalvala was far more than the shower of thin ice crystals that fell constantly throughout the winter.

By the second morning of heavy snowfall Tulo switched on the brown plastic table radio that Pedar had won at the fair years ago. One of the Inari stations, fifty kilometers to the south, was playing Sibelius so he turned the dial to the other just in time to hear ". . . many power lines. More than a meter of snow has fallen in the Inari and Ivalo area, and the low-pressure center seems to be stationary. We caution all residents of the province, especially in the isolated villages of the far north, to remain close to their homes, since the weather bureau now predicts this may be the worst storm to descend upon our land in many years."

Tulo hurriedly dressed in his warmest clothes, hitched Kala to the sledge, and rode off in the darkness. He returned trembling, more than two hours later, with only a small sack of flour and three candles. LaVeeg's store, choked with panic-stricken villagers screaming and pushing and shoving to buy any available supplies, had reminded him of frightened reindeer circling helplessly around the corral at roundup time.

Uncle Varno, who had also been at the store, rode up alongside as Tulo climbed from his sledge. Inside, the stocky herdsman sipped his coffee in silence before he placed his hand on Tulo's shoulder and said, "Your aunt is worried about the two of you. She wants you both to come stay with us, at least until this miserable weather has ended. I told her I would ask even though it would be like talking to the wind."

Tulo shook his head. "We'll be safe, uncle."

"Do not be so confident, nephew. This is a very dangerous storm. I remember one like this when I was your age, but things were different then."

"Different?"

Varno pounded the table, spilling his coffee. "I know, I know—you don't understand. With all your reading and studying you have yet to learn from any of those expensive books how this so-called modern civilization has turned all Same people into soft weaklings who can no longer deal with their own survival as could our fathers and grandfathers." Varno walked to the kerosene stove and pointed to its warm black top with disdain. "What do you do with this contraption?"

Tulo replied, "We cook on it and it also helps to keep us warm. It's just like the stove in your house, uncle."

"And how will you keep from freezing when you have no more oil to feed this iron monster and you

35

have burned the last of your small stack of logs in the fireplace?"

"I have never experienced a storm like this before. I don't know what we'll d-d-d-do," Tulo stammered.

"And neither does any other family in Kalvala!" Varno roared. He marched to the kitchen table, reached up, and snapped off the electric light. His voice rumbled in the darkness. "And what will you do when the power lines fall and these little pieces of glass can no longer shine?"

Jaana's faint voice said, "Then we'll light our candles."

"And when your candles are gone, then what? There are no more at the store."

"Then we'll light the kerosene lamps," replied Jaana confidently, as her despairing uncle snapped on the light, causing her to blink.

"Oh, no, you won't! What little oil you have must be conserved for that stove; otherwise you will not only freeze but you will have to eat dried meat instead of hot stews."

"But we have no dried meat!"

"And why not?"

"Because except for our reindeer meat we buy everything we need as we need it, just as you do—at LaVeeg's store."

"But his store is empty, Tulo! You saw that with your own eyes. Everyone rushed there while their sledges could still move, as we did, and bought everything on LaVeeg's shelves. There is no more food and no more kerosene and the supply trucks are not moving from the south. We are helpless, just as helpless as if we lived in a zoo and the keeper had deserted us."

The youngsters remained respectfully silent while their uncle continued.

"We are all caught in the same trap and we have no one to blame but ourselves for this helpless condition we are in. We have chosen to forget the ways of our ancestors, who managed to survive on this land for thousands of years with courage and ingenuity. We have traded our heredity for silly luxuries. Fifty years ago, even twenty-five, every family had its own herd of reindeer, and no Same was beholden to anyone except his family and his God. Now there are only a few herds in the entire province and our people work in mines or factories or power plants, all slaves in chains of our own making. We have exchanged our only valuable possessions—self-reliance, independence, and our animals—for a light bulb, a music box . . . and a warm behind!"

Varno rose and pushed his arms into his coat.

"Someday they will round us all up, put a fence around us, shoot our reindeer, and forget us just as they did the American Indian and his buffalo." He leaned forward and kissed his niece on her nose. "I'm sorry. I did not mean to make a speech or frighten you. Your aunt tells me I have a big mouth. Tomorrow I'll come by, somehow, to make certain that you are both enduring this tribulation with true Same courage."

Jaana and Tulo followed their uncle out to his sledge, lowering their heads against the biting wind. After Varno was seated Jaana leaned close to him and shouted in his ear so that she could be heard above the storm.

"Uncle Varno, what can we do?"

Varno grasped Jaana's snowy head between his large gloved hands and held her close. He spoke only one word into her ear.

"Pray!"

Eight

☆

On the third day of the storm Tulo built a gigantic kite.

By the time Jaana awoke he had cut and trimmed two willow poles, lashed them into a giant cross with braided reindeer sinew, and mounted an old red cotton sheet to the frame.

"That must be the biggest kite in all the world!" Jaana squealed.

Her brother rose to his feet and studied his work proudly. "Oh, no, there have been kites twenty times this size and more."

"What are you going to do with it?"

"I'm going to do what Mama wants me to do."

"Tulo, Mama is dead!"

"Last night I had a dream, and it was so real that it woke me, and then I couldn't sleep again for thinking about it."

"A dream about Mama?"

"In my dream I was in the meadow, near the star tree, and I was flying a big red kite. The wind was strong and the sun was bright and my kite climbed so high I could barely see it. Then I heard someone

39

laughing, and when I turned I saw Mama sitting in the branches of our tree and she was saying, over and over, 'Look up. Reach out.' I let out more and more line, so happy that it was giving her pleasure."

"Oh, I wish I could have a dream like that!"

Tulo raised his hands. "Wait, there is more. Soon there was thunder and lightning and it turned dark and snow began to fall. I tried to pull in the line to save the kite from the storm but it would not come down. I pulled and pulled until I was afraid my line would break, and then I began to cry. Suddenly there was so much light it was like daytime and when I turned toward Mama she was gone . . . but the star tree was shining as if it were on fire."

"That is very sad . . . and beautiful, Tulo."

"Jaana, I believe that Mama and the star tree appeared in my dream with a message. I think I know what it is. I'll tell you in a little while. Just trust me, for now. We must hurry to the village and buy all the twine and thin rope in Mr. LaVeeg's store."

"For our kite?"

"Just trust me. Hurry!"

The entrance to LaVeeg's General Store was mounded high with drifts, and when Tulo and Jaana pushed against the door loose mounds of snow spilled into the store.

"Stupid children! Quickly, quickly, close the door! Can't you see what you're doing to my floor?"

Finn LaVeeg's whiny voice fitted his face and personality. He had lived—friendless, alone, and tolerated by the villagers—in the back of the only general store in Kalvala, for more than forty years.

His bone-rimmed glasses, taped at one corner, rested above his perpetually wrinkled forehead on a mat of yellowish-white unkempt hair. He continued to remove and mark canned goods from a stack of cartons as the children approached.

Tulo exclaimed, "Mr. LaVeeg, my uncle said that your store was empty, but now your shelves are filled with everything!"

LaVeeg coughed nervously and wiped his mouth on the corner of his stained apron. "What does Varno know? I've been saving these goods in the hut behind my store for a long time. I knew . . . oh, yes, I knew that sooner or later we would have a storm like this and all supplies would be at a premium. One must look ahead. One must prepare for the worst at all times. And they'll pay for these, oh, yes! They'll pay. I'm doubling the price on everything. Supply and demand, demand and supply, you know."

He continued to mark each article with his grease crayon, chuckling aloud as he scrawled his numbers, forgetting that he was not alone. Jaana followed her brother to the shelf displaying rope and twine, and the two began carrying every ball and skein to the counter near the cash register.

LaVeeg finally looked up and groaned. "Now what are you two doing?"

They chorused, "We're buying rope."

"What for? Why do you need so much?"

Tulo paled, not having anticipated, as he knew he should have, that such an unusual purchase would arouse the storekeeper's curiosity. Jaana immediately sensed his dilemma and replied demurely, "I'm going to braid many belts and knit sweaters and shawls for us to sell, next summer, when we have our tent next to the highway."

LaVeeg grunted. "You're going there again, without your mother?"

"Yes."

"Foolishness. You'll lose everything. What do you two know about commerce and finance? Oh, well, that's not my worry. I have more rope and some reindeer thread in the attic. Do you want that too? I won't even mark up the price if you take it all."

Tulo hesitated. He had half their total savings with him. He nodded.

Hours later, surrounded by balls of yarn, rope, and sinew piled high around the red kite, the two sat exhausted before the fireplace staring into the flames from the last of their logs.

"Tulo, you promised . . . and I cannot wait any longer. Please tell me what all this has to do with your dream. Are you going to fly your pretty kite in this storm?"

Tulo looked into the trusting blue eyes of his young sister and struggled for words that would help her to understand. "Soon our supply of oil and candles will be gone, like the logs, and Uncle Varno says that it is only a matter of time before the storm knocks down the electric lines. Jaana, we are not lemmings. We cannot survive, as they do, in total darkness and freezing cold until spring. I am positive that Mama, somehow, is still watching over us."

"How?"

"I believe she came to me, in my dream last

night, to tell me to send up a special kite, large and strong, which I have made."

"Why, Tulo? How will flying a kite save us?"

Tulo stood and pointed at the huge cloth diamond. "This kite will be our net. Tomorrow we are going fishing with it, high in the sky, until we catch a star . . . a star that will give us light and heat for our cabin until spring comes and the sun returns!"

Throughout the night, while the people of Kalvala slept with their fears, Tulo and Jaana Mattis frantically tied rope and twine into a giant ball as they prepared for their assault on heaven.

Nine

In the early hours of the fourth day of the storm, the children hauled their immense kite through the snow to the meadow, its long white-ribboned tails flapping noisily in the wind like the fins of a beached salmon.

Earlier Tulo had rolled the giant ball of rope and twine to a windswept spot close to their tree, and now he knelt and quickly knotted its leading end of line to the kite bridles. Satisfied, he nodded to Jaana, who retrieved their lantern and stepped back.

Almost immediately a violent blast of frigid air ripped across the meadow, scattering loose snow with the force of a giant snowplow. Tulo leaped to his feet, raised the huge kite by its spine, and with all his strength pushed it away from his small body. As if it were no more than a dried birch leaf, the red kite was swept aloft and its fluttering tails quickly disappeared into the murky blackness above.

Meter after meter of line raced through Tulo's fingers. His heart pounded as the rope vibrated and tore at the palms of his gloves. Up sped the line while Jaana furiously unwound more from the gradually shrinking ball. Tulo braced his legs and dug his boots into the slippery underfooting, amazed that this kite seemed to be rising uninterruptedly without striking any of the downdrafts that always kept every kite flier on the alert.

By the time Jaana tugged on her brother's sleeve, after more than two hours had passed, every part of Tulo's body ached. His mending knee felt as if it would give way at any moment, his arms were numb, and his fingers burned. He shook his head helplessly when Jaana pointed to their ball of rope, which had now shrunk to less than one tenth its original size. Like the experienced fisherman he was, Tulo continued to ease out line, even with the realization that disaster was only moments away. If he reached the end of their twine and the kite continued to climb he would be faced with only two choices: hold the line tightly in his grasp until it snapped or pulled him aloft, or release his grip and loose the kite.

Tulo's small gloved hands, through which he now fed rope grudgingly, came together as they did when he prayed at his bedside each night. As he had heard his mother do, so many times, he began to whisper, "Please help me. Please help me." A quick glance at Jaana's anguished face warned him that their supply of rope was nearing its end.

Suddenly the line ceased racing through his hands. The pull from above stopped. Tulo tugged lightly on the rope, checking for a possible downdraft. The line refused to give. Again he tugged, this time with more pressure.

"What is it, Tulo? What's wrong?"

"I don't know!" he yelled above the wind. "The kite doesn't seem to be moving upward any more, but it's not falling either. I wish I could see it. Every time I pull on the line it pulls back. It could be just the wind, but I'm afraid that if I pull too hard the rope will break. It's just like my dream. It's just like it was in my dream!"

After several moments of indecision Tulo decided to risk everything. He jerked savagely on the line. More than three meters of rope tumbled through his hands. He pulled again. More line fell earthward. Hand over hand he tugged and strained and soon a large pile of rope had accumulated at his feet.

"Look, there's a light, Tulo! I see a light!" shouted Jaana. "And . . . there's our kite with something shiny tangled up in it. Is it a star? Pull, Tulo, pull!"

As the light descended, its radiance caused the tree to cast strange and dancing shadows on the snow. Even their cabin, more than a hundred meters away, was now clearly visible to the children. Keeping a firm grasp on the line, Tulo edged closer to the tree until the kite and its shimmering captive were directly overhead. Carefully he guided the tattered red giant, still struggling to fly, into the branches. The tree's sturdy boughs, which had never supported anything heavier than an occasional gray owl, now wrapped themselves around the glowing visitor from space.

"It's so small and round," cried Jaana. "It *is* a real star, isn't it, Tulo? I thought stars had five points. The ones in church and in my schoolbooks all have five points!"

Tulo, still struggling to understand what he had done, mumbled dazedly, "Stars are probably like people or reindeer or trees and come in many shapes and sizes and colors. I don't know. Look, it seems to be on fire, but the tree's branches are not burning! I can't believe we've done it!"

Tulo climbed the big tree and cut the line that had become entangled in its branches. Then he kicked at the kite until it floated limply to the ground. Now he was within arm's length of the star. He could feel its warmth and his eyes watered from the intensity of its varying green and blue and silver light. He was tempted to reach out and touch it but he dared not.

By the time Tulo was back on the ground the star was pulsating with bursts of gold and silver sparks. Jaana squeezed her hands together and exclaimed, "Now we have a real star tree! We have the only star tree in all the world!"

Tulo shook his head in wonder. "And all its branches are shining . . . just as they were in my dream."

Ten

"Tulo! Tulo! Wake up. Wake up!"

Varno shook his nephew gently until the exhausted boy was conscious enough to reach for the cord hanging above his bed. He pulled on it. He pulled again . . . and again.

"What has happened to our lights, uncle?"

In the darkness Varno grunted. "I don't know. The power lines have probably fallen as I warned you they would. But that's not why I'm here."

"What's the matter, uncle?"

"What's the matter, you ask? Here you are sleeping and the world could come to an end without your knowing it. For all I know this may be the end! Hurry! Put something on and follow me."

Tulo dazedly trailed his uncle to the back door, swaying sleepily while Varno wrestled with the latch. When the door flew open the youth blinked several times before his eyes became adjusted to the glare.

"Uncle, why are all those people in our meadow?"

"Why? Why? Are you blind? Look at what is in your tree!"

"That's our star."

"Your star?" bellowed Varno.

"That's our star," Tulo repeated calmly. "We caught it last night."

"You caught it? You . . . caught . . . a star?"

Varno knelt to study his nephew's face in the vivid glow that filled the cabin. He shook his head, rose, walked to the kitchen table, and slumped down next to Jaana, who had been awakened by their voices.

"One of you, please . . . please tell me about this . . . this star."

As the young people spoke, frequently interrupting each other, their uncle's head swung from side to side, his forehead creased by a deep scowl, his mouth repeatedly opening and closing. When they finished he asked, "Where is this great kite of yours?"

"In the barn."

Varno was gone no more than five minutes. When he returned his manner and voice had softened considerably. "And what do you plan to do with this prize catch of yours?"

"We are going to place it there, on the hearth, so that it can light and warm our cabin through this storm and the dark time. Aren't you proud of us, uncle?" Tulo asked. "It is not easy to catch a star."

"Not easy, you say? Oh, no, not easy. Impossible! Impossible, that's all! What can I say? Who ever thought we would see a miracle in this forgotten part of the world? I don't understand. I don't understand any of it."

The simple people of Kalvala rejoiced when they were told the extraordinary news. Old women fell to their knees with prayers of gratitude; young couples held hands and sang while children danced and played as if they were at the fair. Everyone, their plight momentarily forgotten, welcomed with open hearts what Pastor Bjork said was a light sent from God.

Many hours later, after the villagers had finally departed and Jaana was asleep, Tulo was describing the bewildering events of the past twenty-four hours in his green ledger when he felt an uncontrollable urge to return to the meadow. He dressed quickly and went.

The meadow, because it was on a slight rise, had been swept nearly clear of snow by strong winds. Surrounding the tree were patches of yellow and gray reindeer moss where even the ice had melted. Tulo limped under the boughs and reached upward so that he could feel the star's warmth. Falling snowflakes turned to raindrops in the palms of his hands.

"Hello, Tulo."

Startled, the youth spun around in a full circle, wondering who had remained in the meadow. He saw no one.

"Hello, Tulo," said a deep resonant voice once more. "Don't be frightened. Look up!"

Tulo grasped the tree trunk for support and stared up at the star, stammering. "Y-y-y-you can talk?"

"Of course."

"And you know my n-n-name?"

"I know a good deal about you, young man."

"How do you speak? I can't see any mouth."

A shower of silver sparks erupted from the top of the iridescent ball and floated lazily to the ground. "I'm afraid you're thinking of me as if I were an earth person, which obviously I am not. As a star my voice is merely a small part of the energy I radiate."

"Can you see me?"

"Quite clearly. I do have all the senses you have, but that's not unusual since we're all made from the same matter. I even have feelings and moods like you. I cry . . . I laugh . . . I have good moments and bad."

"Do you have a name?"

"Certainly. I've been called Acabar ever since I was formed. Let's see, that would be about one hundred thousand of your years ago."

Already Tulo was completely at ease with his celestial visitor—as if conversing with a star were an everyday matter. He smiled and rolled the strange name on his tongue impishly. "Acabar-r-r-r! Acabar-r-r-r! If you are so old why are you so small?"

Acabar's color reddened. "I'm small because I'm a very young star. In a few trillion years I'll be as large as those stars you earth people have named Capella and Pollux and Arcturus—even Vega. However, I can assure you that neither my youth nor my size is a handicap in the performance of my duties."

"Do all stars talk?"

"In countless languages, but the larger ones are

so far away from each other that they rarely have an opportunity. Loneliness is one of the prices they must pay for greatness. Smaller stars like myself, able to move about at will, are very important up there. You've seen us flying across the sky now and then, I know. We're always rushing somewhere to help out in any way we can. That's why I'm here now."

Tulo was stunned. "You mean you came here to help *me?*"

"Yes."

"My kite. You . . . you let me catch you in my kite?"

"Of course. All the rope on this planet of yours would not have been enough to reach me if I didn't want to be caught, but that's not to take anything away from your marvelous handling of that red devil. You were superb."

Tulo spun around with glee, nearly losing his balance. "Thank you, Star Acabar, thank you! How wonderful you are to travel all the way down here just to help me warm and light our cabin during this terrible time!"

The star's color diminished to a soft blue before he replied. "Little man, I did not come for that—although I am willing to serve you in that capacity also, if you wish. Actually, I have come with a gift for you . . . a gift that will be more valuable than a little temporary light and heat for your cabin."

Tulo circled the tree slowly, squinting at the shining ball from all sides.

"Gift? I don't see it."

A thunderous laugh shook the star tree. "My

gift is not wrapped in pretty paper and tied with a ribbon, if that's what you're looking for, Tulo. Just be patient and I'll try to explain. You know, from your studies in school, that this earth is just a small planet among a huge galaxy of stars that earth people call the Milky Way. Well, there are more than a billion other galaxies out there, so many that it even boggles my mind when I think about it. In this galaxy alone there are over one hundred billion stars . . . and more than one hundred million planets with life on them—"

"I didn't know that!" Tulo interrupted.

"Of course you didn't. Earth people still have much to learn. However, for reasons we have never questioned, of all the planets with life in the entire universe, earth is the only one where people have been given a very special power: the power of choice. Only here, no matter how desperate your circumstances may be, are you allowed to influence your own destiny through the choices you make. Here you can choose to be kind or hateful, courageous or cowardly, rich or poor, lazy or industrious, sinful or holy . . . and of course suffer the consequences or reap the rewards for your actions. No one has ever been born on this planet without that power since the days of the Garden of Eden."

"I know about Adam and Eve!"

Acabar's light pulsated rapidly. "Well, ever since those two made the wrong choice we have watched your actions down here with great interest . . . and disappointment. When confronted with two choices people usually make the wrong one. Although there have been millions, through the centuries, who have used their power wisely, the majority choose to spend so much of their precious allotment of life feeling sorry for themselves that they have no time to enjoy the paradise that was created here. Humans, I'm sorry to say, do not know how to live. All they can do well is die . . . a little each day. You, Tulo, are no better than the others."

"Me?"

"You! Recall all the self-pity you have lavished on yourself during the past year and tell me I am wrong!"

"Your gift for me will help me to change? It will teach me how to live?"

"My gift will do nothing for you unless you are willing to work at changing yourself. A life must change from within."

"You sound like Mama."

"I've known you as long as your mother. I've been your special star and watched over you since you were born. I suffered with you . . . and I triumphed with you as you learned the art of writing. Then you had that accident and gave up on life just as so many earth people do when life mistreats them. My gift is for you . . . and for all others who believe their lives here are a failure because they are unable to climb the highest mountain or fill a warehouse with gold."

Acabar's words frightened Tulo. All he had wanted was a tiny star to give light and heat to their small cabin. He replied so softly that his words could scarcely be heard above the moaning wind.

"Star Acabar, have you ever come to earth before?"

The star shimmered in silence.

"Star Acabar?"

"Yes, yes, I heard you. I was just trying to decide whether or not to reply. But then, no one will believe you anyway if you tell them that we've talked to each other."

"My sister will . . . as soon as she hears you."

"Ah, but she won't hear me, Tulo. A star can only be heard by his own special earth person."

Tulo persisted. "Please tell me anyway, Star Acabar. Please! Have you been here before?"

The star's glow diminished and he replied, with an obvious note of pride, "Yes, I flew down here once on a very, very special mission. I was selected and dispatched to earth, many of your years ago, to locate a small cave behind a dingy inn in a place that was somewhere around thirty-two degrees north latitude and thirty-five degrees east longitude, as I recall. After I found it my orders were to do what most other stars would never dare attempt: I was to remain in a fixed position, only a thousand meters above the cave, and put forth my brightest light for seven days and seven nights. Then I was free to return. It was extremely difficult . . . but I did it!"

Tulo's voice broke when he asked, "How long ago, Star Acabar?"

"I would say about two thousand earth years ago."

"And do you remember the name of the place?"

"I shall never forget it. It was a small village, just about the size of this one, except that it was on a desert. Its name was Bethlehem."

Eleven

☆

Jaana waited until her brother, weary from a night of writing in his green ledger, had filled himself on glowing cake before she said, "Tulo, I slept very little, thinking about our star. It does not seem right that soon we shall have the only light and heat in Kalvala."

"It is only one small star," Tulo replied. "It cannot possibly serve every home in the village. Besides, all our wood is gone, there is no electricity, and we only have candles and oil for a few more days."

"But already there are many families without oil or candles, and that horrible LaVeeg has raised his prices so much they cannot afford to buy more. What about them?"

Tulo walked toward the door, pretending not to hear. "When Uncle Varno comes, tell him that I'm in the meadow so that we can make our plans to move Acabar into the cabin."

"Move who?"

"The star."

"You called it Ac—Aca—Acabar. Have you given it a name already?"

Tulo escaped without answering and limped through the meadow to the big tree with its shining occupant.

"Good morning, little man. Dark clouds seem to be covering your fair countenance. Is something wrong?"

"Good morning, Star Acabar. It's my sister. She thinks I'm selfish for wanting to keep you in our cabin when so many others need you more than we do."

"And you're upset because you know that what she says is true and now your conscience is bothering you. No accuser lives who is as powerful as the conscience which dwells within us."

After several moments of silence Acabar continued.

"Speaking of conscience, why are you no longer writing those lovely poems and stories that you did so well? Why are you wasting your talent by not using it?"

Tulo lowered his head so that he would not have to face his inquisitor. He kicked at the snow, shrugged his shoulders, and replied dolefully, "What's the use? I'm a cripple, with little education, and now there will never be any money for me to attend the university. What I write is unimportant. No one has ever paid any attention to a Same poet, anyway. Mama and I had many wonderful plans, but they were all too good to be true."

Acabar erupted with a prolonged shower of red sparks. "Nothing is too good to be true! That's the same kind of self-pity we've been hearing for thousands of years from just about every part of this planet. You earth people are certainly fortunate that not everyone chooses to give up in the face of adversity, or you would have all disappeared a long time ago. And what do you plan to do about your debt?"

Surprised by the star's harsh words, Tulo responded defiantly, "Debt? I owe no one, not even LaVeeg!"

"Ah, but you do, little man! Along with the power of choice you received the most precious gift our Creator can bestow: the spark of life. With it came an obligation to apply your own special talents, whatever they may be, to leave this world a better place than you found it. Billions of humans have failed in this obligation and wasted their lives. On the other hand, if you use your talent and repay your debt—"

Tulo could not contain himself. "What will happen, what will happen, Star Acabar?"

"Repay your debt, give something of yourself to your world each day, and your life here will be filled with harmony and satisfaction and love, followed by a joyful eternity in the Kingdom of Forever."

Tulo frowned. "I have never heard of the Kingdom of Forever."

"I know you haven't. Earth people are still infants when it comes to universal knowledge. Look up, son! Look directly over your head."

For the first time in more than a week the stars suddenly became visible. Tulo stared into the heavens and waited for Acabar's next words.

"See that bright star to the left? That is Louis Pasteur. Have you studied about Pasteur?"

"Yes."

"And that star to Pasteur's left, see it?"

"Yes."

"That is Seneca. Do you know of that great Roman?"

"Oh, yes. I have studied many of his wise sayings!"

"Then your time with books has not been wasted. Now, look toward your cabin. See that star just above the chimney?"

"Yes."

"Galileo. And next to him is Benjamin Franklin."

"He flew kites, too!"

"Ah, yes, so he did. Almost got himself killed one night. But I assure you he's up there for more than his kite flying."

"Star Acabar, you mean that all I have to do to become a shining star in the Kingdom of Forever is use the talent that God has given me to make this a better world?"

"My son, we've been trying to get through to earth with that simple message for thousands of years. And yet, more and more humans are born, grow up, and die, believing that their life has no purpose, no meaning, and no plan. To them our magnificent universe, filled with order and design, is just an accident. No wonder they have so little courage to face life's adversities."

"Whee!" Tulo yelled, leaping so high that he cracked his head on the lowest branch of the tree. Ignoring his throbbing knee he raced around the star tree in short circles, pointing to one star and then another. Each time he pointed, Acabar announced another name in this strangest of all roll calls: "Joan of Arc . . . Thomas Edison . . . Mahatma Gandhi . . . Shakespeare . . . Marco Polo . . . Inga Mattis . . ."

"Who?" Tulo's body became rigid, his hand still pointing skyward.

"Inga Mattis. That star you're pointing to is your mother. Why are you surprised, Tulo?"

"My mother? B-but she's not famous like the others you named. How is it that she . . .?"

"My dear boy," Acabar blazed, "it is obvious that you are not paying attention. It is not necessary that you be wealthy or famous or a genius in order to fulfill your own destiny. All that is asked is that you use whatever gifts you have to the best of your ability. If your skill is with a hammer, build! If you have a knack with a hoe, plant! If you are happy on the water, fish! If a pen does your bidding, write!"

Tears rolled unashamedly down Tulo's cheeks as he reached up with both arms toward the tiny twinkling star. "Mama . . . Mama!"

"Yes, and if you look closely you will see your father next to her. This planet is certainly a better place because of those two honest, hard-working people who never wasted a moment feeling sorry for themselves."

Acabar's words were almost more than Tulo's young mind could comprehend. He fell to his knees. "But what can I possibly do to make this a better world? Even to survive here is a struggle."

"How fortunate you are," beamed Acabar.

Tulo hung his head. "Now you are making fun of me, Star Acabar."

"No, I'm not, little poet. If you had been born in luxury you wouldn't have this marvelous opportunity to make yourself strong and resourceful through your own effort. To struggle is the only certain way for anyone to achieve his full potential. Did your mother give up when your father was taken from you? No! You should have learned from her example. Instead, you've done little but heap pity on yourself!"

"I can't help it. I do try, but life seems so hopeless for me. I can't even walk like other people."

Acabar's voice was like thunder. "There are other stars up there, stars like Beethoven, who was deaf . . . Milton, who was blind . . . and Lincoln, who lived in terrible poverty, far worse than yours. Hear me, Tulo! Adversity is not a curse, it is a blessing. The brightest stars in heaven are those who have been tested in the furnace of tribulation. Show me a human being who has never suffered adversity and I'll show you the most unhappy person on earth!"

Slowly the star's color turned a deep blue and his voice was soft as he continued.

"Tulo, you live in a world filled with people making excuses for their failure because it is always easier to quit than to keep trying. I cannot allow you to walk that path of despair. I came here to help you live at peace with yourself so that you can fulfill your own destiny with pride and a contented heart. And you will—if you heed my words and also make good use of my gift."

61

"Your gift. I had almost forgotten. . . ."

"Tulo, my gift to you is such a small and simple thing that I'm afraid few earth people will ever recognize its value or its power. It is simply a collection that I began ages ago as I watched the endless parade of humanity marching from cradle to grave with no light to guide them while the words of your great philosophers and prophets were ignored and lost forever to future generations. I decided to do something to correct this wrong, so I began preserving the wisdom from the greatest minds who have ever lived here. Then, after a thousand years or so, I made an amazing discovery."

Tulo remained silent, listening eagerly.

"I discovered that the wisest, most contented and productive humans, even when separated by continents and centuries, conducted their lives as if they were all being guided by different laws from the rest of humanity. I assembled their principles and secrets for a good and tranquil life into a brief list and gave it a name: Credenda."

"C-Credenda? What does that mean, Star Acabar?"

"Forgive me, Tulo, but I've always been partial to the language of Seneca and Cicero. Credenda is a Latin word for matters of faith or doctrines to be believed. It's from their verb 'credere,' which means to trust or believe."

"Credenda," Tulo repeated. "It sounds very strange and . . . and magical."

"True. It does sound strange because it is a word that has rarely been used on this planet for centuries. But the magic, Tulo, the magic is already within you . . . within all humans! Credenda is only the key that will unlock the best that is in everyone, providing they take its words to their heart every day. It is yours—providing you fulfill two requests."

"Anything, Star Acabar, anything!"

"Hold your tongue until you hear what I ask. First, because I know you are not a selfish person, you must go to the leaders of your village and tell them you would like me placed wherever they decide it will benefit the greatest number of people in Kalvala. Inform them that you will abide by their decision providing they agree to transport me back here to this lovely and special tree as soon as the sun returns, so that I can be attached to your kite and returned to the heavens. You see, Tulo, unlike my last visit when I floated free above the cave, this time I am unable to release myself from the bonds of earth without your help. Will you do this for me . . . and yourself?"

Tulo pressed his small face against the rough tree bark. His nod was almost imperceptible.

"I'm certain, little friend, that you have the courage and charity to carry out my wish, for you know in your heart that it is the right thing to do. Now for my second request. You keep a diary, do you not, in that green ledger you received when you were recovering from your accident?"

"Yes. How did you . . . ? Oh, I forgot. You know everything about me."

"Tomorrow, when you return from your village leaders, bring the green ledger here. I shall recite every word of Credenda to you so that you can inscribe it in your ledger. The words are few, and we should be able to complete the transcription before they come to move me. Later, after I am gone, it is my greatest wish that you find some way to share Credenda with the world so that many others will have the same opportunity to live a life of harmony as I shall give to you. Is this also agreeable to you?"

"Yes, Star Acabar, I will do everything you ask."

"Very well, it is settled. Now I must rest. I have not talked so much at one time in all my life, and I'm afraid my energy level is very low. Still, I shall be at full strength for you tomorrow. Good day, Tulo. I love you very much, little man."

"I love you, too, Star Acabar."

The light from the star tree guided Tulo back to the cabin, where he told a happy Jaana of his decision to give their star to the people. Then he sat at the kitchen table and rehearsed for the next day by writing down in the green ledger every word he could remember of his conversation with Acabar.

Tulo closed his entry, dated December 17, with:

Now I understand why there are so many stars in the sky.

How thoughtful of God to assign a different one to watch over each of us. If everyone knew this secret surely they would never lose hope or feel lonely as long as they lived.

I have learned so much today, yet there is one thing I do not understand. Why do I, of all the billions of people in this world, have as my special star the same one that watched over the little cave in Bethlehem so very long ago?

Why?

Twelve

☆

Tuntu Van Gribin, chairman of the Kalvala village council, ushered his apprehensive visitors into a large wallpapered room brilliantly illuminated by eight thick candles, three oil lamps, and a crackling fireplace.

The mayor, a title Van Gribin had assumed unofficially, squeezed his round frame into a wicker chair facing Tulo and Jaana and wheezed. "My, my, this is indeed an honor. To think I have as my guests the only people in the entire world who own their own star. Amazing . . . amazing! I wish that I could visit with you at length. However, we are holding a council meeting here, within the hour, to explore whatever steps we can take to deal with this terrible crisis which has befallen us. Food and oil supplies in most homes are very low, candles are as rare as diamonds, and the power cables are now buried under tons of snow. We are a life raft in an ocean of terror. Terrible . . . terrible. However, we shall find a way, never fear, never fear. Now, tell me what you nice children are doing here when you have such a comforting treasure in your meadow?"

Tulo timidly rubbed his wet boots through the giant black bear rug beneath his chair and mumbled, "Sir, we have come to offer our star to the village so that everyone can share its light."

"What?" Van Gribin exclaimed. "I cannot believe my ears. You two are willing to give up your precious star for the good of the village?"

Both children nodded.

"This is amazing, almost as great a miracle as the star's being here at all! And where would you like your star to be placed?"

Tulo shook his head. "We don't know, sir. We shall leave that up to you."

"Oh, no, no, not up to me! Certainly not up to me. But wait." Van Gribin beamed. "The council members will soon be here. Let them decide. That is the official way—and legal too, I'm sure. Yes, yes, we'll let the council decide. I still can't believe it! My, my!"

The other members of the village council were Finn LaVeeg, the store owner, Pastor Erno Bjork, of the church, Arrol Nobis, the schoolmaster, and Hjorta Malni, the only physician within many kilometers of Kalvala.

After everyone was seated around Van Gribin's long dining table, with Tulo and Jaana huddled close to each other at the far end, the mayor called the meeting to order, dispensed with all other business, and dramatically announced the priceless donation their village had just received from his two young guests.

Loud applause continued until Van Gribin

pounded the table for silence and said, in his best chairman's voice, "The chair is now open for suggestions from the esteemed council as to the most beneficial placement of the star. Pastor Bjork, would you kindly commence the discussion?"

The pastor stood, raised his fleshy arms as if he were still in his pulpit, and directed his remarks toward the children. "Friends, we are supremely blessed, this day, to share in one of the most noble acts ever witnessed on this earth. That these two beautiful children, whose parents we all knew and loved, should come here of their own free will and offer their greatest possession to their neighbors, with no thought of reward or recompense, is charity and love of the highest order."

Jaana glanced uncertainly at Tulo, who shrugged his shoulders as the pastor continued.

"I grant you that we have here the five individuals, including myself, who in one way or another serve every soul in Kalvala. Still, with all due respect to this council I believe the decision as to where the star is to be located should be made by no one but its owners, Tulo and Jaana Mattis."

LaVeeg, the store owner, glowered and muttered under his breath, but the others remained respectfully silent as Pastor Bjork concluded.

"I move that each member state his preference as to the star's new location, along with his reasoning for such a choice. Then let the children decide —and I move that we abide by their decision."

Arrol Nobis responded immediately. "I second both motions!"

Finn LaVeeg jumped to his feet without waiting

to be called. He stared at the two young people and forced his lips into a half smile until two yellow teeth protruded. His voice was almost a whine as he reminded the gathering, again and again, of the importance of his store to village life and his inability to serve his customers properly in the dark. He closed his long soliloquy by smashing the table with his bony fist and demanding, "You must allow the star to light my great store or the life of this village is doomed!"

In contrast, Arrol Nobis gave a calm and brief review of the value of education and his inability to teach the children without light. He patiently explained that each lost day of learning could never be regained and closed his remarks by saying, "I ask for your star, not for myself but for tomorrow's citizens. You have it in your power to provide them with the precious light of knowledge."

Dr. Malni appeared embarrassed at having to speak but he haltingly reminded the group that his small clinic provided the only medical care for the village. He cited the lives that had been saved and the babies that had been delivered in the past year and even touched on the work that had been performed on Tulo's knee. He ended by stating, "Our clinic will soon be in total darkness. Should my services be needed, the star's light in my clinic may make the difference between life and death for someone."

Pastor Bjork was the last to speak. He spoke of the miracle that had blessed their land and the hand of God that had directed Tulo's kite to the small star. His church, he mourned, which should be a refuge for all in these perilous times, was empty and dark, since he had distributed nearly all his candles and oil to those in need. He inhaled deeply and bowed his head toward Tulo and Jaana. "I ask you most humbly to place God's miracle in God's house—your church."

All eyes now turned toward the young people. Tulo glanced desperately at his sister, who seemed as if she were about to break into tears. She bit her lip and whispered helplessly, "I don't know what to do. I don't know."

In the torturous minutes that followed, Mayor Van Gribin's contented smile gradually faded when it became obvious that Tulo and Jaana were unable to come to a decision. Finally he snapped his fingers loudly and announced, "People, I believe I have the answer. My long years of experience in matters of conciliation tell me that there is only one solution to our problem. Obviously the children are finding it more difficult to reject three of you than was anticipated so I propose"—he paused dramatically—"I propose that we please everyone by dividing the star into four equal pieces! In that way the entire community, through the school, the church, the clinic, and the store, will share an equal amount of light during these dark days. Less . . . but equal! With ropes and pulleys we can easily remove the star from the tree, and then with hammer and chisel we'll create four stars from one and all parties will be satisfied!" The mayor slumped in his seat, gasping for breath.

"No!" Tulo's cry pierced the room. "Never! The star is not to be broken or it will not be able to take its place in heaven again. When the dark time has ended I am going to attach it to my kite and return it to its home in the sky. It is not ours to keep, and it is entitled to its chance to grow just as much as we are!"

Mayor Van Gribin curled his lips and huffed. "It is only a small piece of rock which happens to be on fire. You talk as if it were alive. I'm afraid you've read too many fairy tales, young man."

LaVeeg angrily pushed himself away from the table and stomped toward the frightened children until his long, crooked forefinger waved close to their strained faces. "Do you two intend to keep the star for that sorry cabin you call a home when so many others could benefit from it? How selfish you are!" The store owner turned and pointed angrily toward the mayor. "And why are we wasting all this precious time begging a couple of stupid orphans for something that belongs to the entire village?"

"The s-s-s-star belongs to us," Tulo cried.

"Oh, no, it doesn't," screamed LaVeeg. He nodded toward Arrol Nobis. "Has not your brilliant schoolteacher, here, taught you about 'eminent domain'?"

Two small blond heads shook vigorously.

"Ha! Well, eminent domain is the right of government to take any private property for public use, with proper compensation to the owner. I propose, gentlemen of the council, that we seize the star by writ of eminent domain and—"

"Why don't you all share the star in another way?" A small voice interrupted the old merchant's tirade. Every head turned toward Jaana, who smiled and continued. "Each of you take the star for two weeks, and by then the sun will have re-

70

turned. You can even draw straws to see who has it first."

The only sound in the room came from the burning logs in the fireplace. Then Pastor Bjork clasped his hands together and whispered hoarsely, "Out of the mouths of babes. We have been witness, once again, to the truth that all children are God's apostles, sent to teach us love, charity, self-denial, compassion, and hope. Kalvala has been truly blessed, this day. I move that we accept the suggestion of Jaana Mattis, whose wisdom far exceeds her years."

The motion was seconded and carried, and to everyone's displeasure, except his own, Finn LaVeeg won the drawing. The star would light his store for fourteen days, followed by the school, then the clinic, and finally the church. All arrangements were completed for the star to be moved on the following day.

On their return home, Tulo and Jaana lowered their heads as they approached their cabin. They could not bring themselves to look toward their meadow.

Despite his grief, Tulo wrote everything down in the green ledger.

Thirteen

☆

The storm subsided on its eighth day and a pallid half-moon greeted the early risers of Kalvala. Still there was no rejoicing in the stricken village. More than half their reindeer had already perished from starvation, unable to dig through the massive accumulation of snow to reach the life-sustaining moss below.

Tulo, carrying his green ledger, returned to the meadow as soon as he awoke. Acabar was silent until the youth stood directly under the tree.

"My, my. You look extremely dejected, I must say, for one who is about to inscribe the first earthly copy of Credenda. I rather expected that seeing all my centuries of research finally being put on paper, even if not on parchment, would be a thrilling experience. Now I'm not so sure."

Tulo dropped his green ledger against the tree and replied dejectedly, "They are coming for you today, Star Acabar."

"Oh ho, I should have known. It's quite difficult for me to keep on top of events from this low altitude. So you did it? You kept your first promise to me?"

Tulo nodded. "The store and the church and the school and the clinic will each have you for two weeks before I fly you back into the sky with my kite."

"Excellent! That sounds like a brilliant solution to a difficult dilemma."

"It was Jaana's idea. They wanted to divide you into four parts."

"Thank you both, for saving my life. Now, don't look so sad. We'll still be able to see each other every day."

"I can't help it, Star Acabar. I know we are doing the right thing but I just cannot bear the thought of giving you up. First Papa, then Mama . . . and now you. I want you near because you are my best friend. It wouldn't matter to me if you had no light or heat. I would give up anything, even your gift, if I could keep you close to me."

The star's color subsided to a dark pink. "Please don't cry, little friend. I am very proud of your act of unselfishness. It is not easy to be unselfish on this planet. Humans fail more often in this area than any other, little realizing that when they do they trade all their tomorrows for dust. Well, you certainly kept your part of our bargain, so let me keep mine before they arrive. Are you prepared to take down Credenda?"

Tulo nodded and opened his green ledger to the first blank page. As he removed his pencil from an inside pocket he cocked his head and asked, "Star Acabar, if I live by the words of your gift will they make me rich and famous?"

A towering fountain of multicolored sparks erupted from Acabar. "Young man, this above all you must learn! Wealth and fame are as fleeting as the wind, and those things doomed to perish bring pleasure to no one. Whatever you want from life, never forget that any goal is futile if you must work hard to get it—and then harder to keep it. Man will never be happy until he ceases his fruitless search for the philosopher's stone."

Tulo was puzzled. "In all of my reading I never learned about the philosopher's stone."

The sparks ceased falling. "It is supposed to be a magic substance that will enable the finder to change base metals, like lead and copper, into gold and silver. Happiness and contentment, it is believed, are certain to follow. Ridiculous! The greatest lie that has ever circulated on this planet is that money can make you happy! The second greatest lie is that success and fame are worth any sacrifice."

"Star Acabar, where is this . . . this philosopher's stone?"

"There is no philosopher's stone!" the star roared, causing the tree to tremble. "There has never been an easy path to the good life that does not violate the laws of nature, and whenever you violate those laws, I promise . . . you are doomed. Enough of that! Let us begin our work, you and I."

Tulo propped himself against the tree and announced, "I'm ready."

"How symbolic it is that you should preserve Credenda in that book. You may not know this, Tulo, but a ledger is called the 'book of final entry.' In it one records all the debits and credits of a business—and of course my list is no more than a simple guide to help anyone balance the debits and credits of life. Your green ledger will be a perfect chalice for—"

Dancing lights from three oil lanterns suddenly appeared from the dark world beyond the meadow. The youth pushed aside the ledger and leaped to his feet in panic.

"Oh, no. No! Star Acabar, they have come for you already, and we have not even begun! What shall we do, what shall we do?"

The star's reassuring voice replied, "Do what one should always do when faced with any difficult situation. Stand fast. We shall have many hours together after they have moved me. You will still receive my gift. Now make me proud of you. Remain calm."

Before Tulo could reply, Uncle Varno was at his side carrying a large coil of heavy rope, looking both angry and reluctant. Behind Varno stood the four village council members and their smiling mayor.

Varno placed his hand on Tulo's small back. He nodded with a heavy scowl toward the others and said, "They tell me you have given them permission to remove your star. Is that correct?"

"Yes, uncle."

"And the decision to do this was reached by your own free will and choice? No pressure or influence was put upon you by our—our eminent mayor or any of these other gentlemen?"

"Jaana and I decided that we should not keep the star for ourselves when it could help so many others."

Varno shrugged his wide shoulders. "Very well,

we shall proceed. Take your little sister away from this tree so that you will both be safe as we are lifting the star."

"Please be careful, uncle."

Varno smiled. "Careful for myself—or your precious star?"

Both brother and sister watched apprehensively as the mayor and the schoolmaster guided four reindeer until their sledge was directly under the tree. A small hand fit into Tulo's, and he could feel the sobs that shook Jaana's small body as she pressed closer to him.

In the tree Varno carefully looped his rope around the star until it was securely bound. He tied several knots. Then he climbed to the next branch and placed the trailing rope across the limb above, creating a pulley from which the heavy sphere could be lifted from its pine cradle, swung away from the tree, and lowered to the sledge.

Finally Varno signaled to the mayor, and his council members all grasped the rope and pulled. The tree shuddered as its branches relinquished their load. Soon the star was free from the boughs and spinning slowly against the background of ebony-blue sky.

"It looks just like a big Christmas tree decoration," sighed Jaana.

No one else spoke as they watched the star's color vary from silver to red to gold while it swayed gently and majestically in the wind. Tulo clenched his fists as Acabar, inch by inch, was lowered to the sledge.

Suddenly Varno's anguished cry sounded across

the meadow. "Hurry, hurry! The rope is separating! Lower it quickly, quickly!"

Those holding the rope did their best, but their reaction was too slow. Like a giant pendulum the star swayed away from the tree, slipped through the parted strands of fiber, and crashed to the ground in a shower of sparks.

Darkness engulfed the meadow.

"Uncle Varno," screamed Tulo as he stumbled toward the star. "We've killed him, we've killed him! Star Acabar's light is gone. Star Acabar is dead!" He fell across the still-warm gray cinder now half buried in reindeer moss. "Star Acabar, I'm sorry, I'm sorry. You should have remained in the sky. Now you are dead because you wanted to help me. I'm sorry!"

Arrol Nobis was the first to speak while Tulo's small body still lay prostrate on the lifeless star. "Greed is what caused this tragedy," he muttered, looking angrily at LaVeeg.

"Stupidity is a better explanation," whined LaVeeg, pointing his lantern toward the parted ropes.

Pastor Bjork raised his hand—and his voice. "God has spoken. It is another warning to man of the consequences that will befall all of us if we continue to tamper with nature. Our concrete highways desecrate the Almighty's forests, our mines displace His mountains, our factories pollute His air. This star, like all the others in heaven, was a jewel in the hem of God's robe. We had no right to covet it for our lowly purposes. May God forgive us our trespasses!"

"Gentlemen," sighed a somber mayor, "nothing we say will rekindle this lovely star. We cannot make gold dust from ashes. Let us return to our homes and pray that we can find another solution to our crisis."

After the others had departed, Varno approached his nephew and niece, who were still kneeling close to the fallen star. "Children, there is nothing more you can do here. Let me take you home."

Varno lifted Jaana into his arms while Tulo limped to the big tree and found his ledger. Then he returned to the cinder and rubbed his hand across its rough exterior, now cold to his touch.

"Please forgive me, Star Acabar. I told you I wanted to keep you near me even if you had no light or warmth—and now I have my wish, a wish I should never have made. Oh, how I wish that I were dead too."

The star tree moaned in the wind.

Fourteen

☆

While Mayor Van Gribin snored unconcernedly in his overstuffed bed there was little sleep for his council members following the tragic event in the meadow.

Finn LaVeeg, bitterly disappointed at his sudden change of fortune, angrily paced the shadowy aisles of his deserted store, which was dimly lit by two small candles from his dwindling hoard. Now he would never reap the sales and profits he expected before the sun returned and the roads were cleared. He pounded his head against a shelf of canned goods and cursed everyone from the mayor to Tulo Mattis.

Hjorta Malni paid his last visit of the day to the two patients in his small clinic and extinguished both oil lamps, after placing an additional blanket on each bed. Without an emergency he knew his fuel would last for four days, but if the operating room was needed his supply would disappear quickly.

Arrol Nobis sat at his desk in the bleak schoolroom, drawing small stars on a yellow pad while a candle stub flickered toward extinction. His situation seemed hopeless. The school was certain to be closed, officially, and in Kalvala it was the custom to pay their schoolmaster only for the days he taught. "This winter," he mourned, "will be the coldest in many ways."

Erno Bjork sat alone, in his dark church, reviewing the extraordinary circumstances of the past few days. When had the last miracle taken place on this earth? And now what proof did they have for the outside world? No one would believe the word of simple and uneducated villagers who, in typical Same fashion, would probably disclose nothing to outsiders anyway. Of course there was still a half-buried piece of charred rock. He shook his head and prayed for assistance.

LaVeeg was the first to arrive at a possible solution to the crisis, and despite the late hour he pushed his way through the swirling snowdrifts with his sledge and two old reindeer until he arrived at the Mattis cabin.

"Young people," the store owner announced to the two red-eyed children he had rudely awakened, "I have a brilliant answer to our problem. Only I could have conceived it!"

Tulo and Jaana rubbed their eyes and waited patiently.

"You must fly your kite to capture another star! You did it once, so you can certainly do it again. More important, you have all the twine. That was ver-r-ry clever of you to buy up all my rope, otherwise the entire village would be out fishing for stars. Only you can save our village, my boy. Find another star and let me keep it until spring and you will be greatly rewarded. I remember how your mother always spoke of sending you to the university. Bring me a star and I'll share all my winter profits with you, more than enough to pay your tuition for at least a year. What do you say to that?"

Tulo shook his sleepy head in bewilderment. "Another star, Mr. LaVeeg? I don't know . . . I don't know."

"Now, now, you think about it. This is your great opportunity to make something of yourself—and probably your last one. But my offer won't wait. It's already past midnight. You let me know by noon today, do you hear?"

Early in the morning, while the children were still in bed, there was another knock on their door, and when Jaana opened it Pastor Bjork's bulky frame filled the small doorway.

Jaana brewed a pot of coffee. After the cleric had sipped nervously from his cup for several moments, he said, "I wanted to come, children, so that I could personally and privately extend my sympathy to both of you for your great loss. We know that what God gives He may take away, but this wonderful miracle and its hasty withdrawal from us is a mystery we should not question. I have prayed for guidance, and I believe God has answered me. Tulo and Jaana, you must fly your kite again. Send it up into the heavens, and if you catch another star please bring it to the church so that it may provide courage and comfort to our people. Do this and I will repay you, every day of my life, in the only way I can: with constant prayers for your eternal glory."

Less than an hour later Dr. Malni was at the door. He too extended his sympathy and politely inquired about Tulo's knee. Then he continued, "Son, I believe my clinic has served this village well for many years, often without pay. My supply of fuel is very low. Should an unfortunate accident befall someone, as it did to you, Tulo, I would not be able to operate if my clinic were dark. I believe your magnificent kite should fly again. Send it up and let it perform its magic to capture another star —and bring the star to the clinic so that it can brighten the lives of those less fortunate than us."

Tulo smiled awkwardly. "Pastor Bjork has already—"

"The pastor has been here with the same suggestion?"

"Yes, and . . . and Mr. LaVeeg, also."

Dr. Malni's face paled and he reached for his cloak. "I had no idea. Still, I beg of you, please remember our clinic if you decide to try."

Arrol Nobis arrived before noon. His color was gray and his eyes were half closed from lack of sleep. "Tulo, I'll come right to the point. I believe it is mathematically possible, if you do exactly as you did before, to catch another star. I've come to ask that you send up your kite again . . . for the schoolchildren who are your friends and classmates."

Tulo's intended reply was cut short by the young schoolmaster, who raised his palms for silence as he did in his classroom.

"Tulo, catch a new star for the children, and I will do everything in my power to see that you are enrolled at the university on a scholarship next year. I have influence and friends there. I'll even tutor you so that you can pass the entrance examination."

The schoolmaster made a hasty departure, leaving behind two speechless pupils.

Early in the afternoon there was one more visitor. Uncle Varno, the glow from his heavy lantern reflecting brightly on his puzzled features, stood in the doorway and pointed toward the dark meadow.

"Have you been down to your star tree today, nephew?"

"No. Why?"

Varno smiled mysteriously. "Both of you, put on some warm clothes and come with me."

Their uncle walked ahead, taking care to shine his lantern only on the snow-packed path immediately before them. When they finally arrived at a slight rise, no more than forty meters from the tree, Varno swung the lantern toward the base of the trunk, exclaiming, "Look! Look . . . and wonder!"

It seemed to Tulo as if every surviving reindeer from their meager herds had gathered, crouching in rows that circled the tree, each animal staring at the gray cinder beneath it with such concentration that even the harsh beam from Varno's lantern did not disturb them.

Jaana whispered, "Listen, Tulo. They're not even grunting as they always do. I hear only the wind."

"Why are they doing that, uncle?" Tulo asked.

Varno shrugged and shook his head. "You're the miracle maker. I thought you might know. I've been around reindeer all my life and I've never seen them act this way. It is almost as if they have gathered to pay their respects to that fallen star of yours—something they never do for their own who die. Look at them! If a wolf were to charge into that herd this moment, I doubt that any would even blink. It is all beyond me, like everything else of this past week, but if that cinder causes our animals to act this way perhaps we should bury it."

"No!" both children cried.

Tulo moved closer, among the reindeer, until he was under the star tree. He reached down and gently caressed the embedded cinder. The rough-textured exterior seemed to give under his touch. He knelt and placed the palms of both hands on its rounded sides.

"Tulo! Tulo!" Varno's impatient call broke the young man's meditation. He limped back to the other two and Varno asked, "Well, what should we do? After all, it is your . . . your star."

Now Tulo's voice was firm and filled with confidence. "I know what to do. Reindeer are very wise animals. I believe they came here with a message they knew I would understand."

"Tulo, please," groaned Varno. "That is crazy talk. Your head is filled with all those silly legends and Christmas folk tales that you have read. A reindeer is just a reindeer."

Tulo looked up at the star-filled sky and repeated, "I know what to do."

"Tell us, please."

"I'm going to fly my kite again . . . and if it is God's will we shall find another star to shine on Kalvala."

Fifteen

☆

Loud cheers and cries of encouragement from the villagers greeted the trio when they appeared in the meadow.

"Maybe we should have charged admission," grunted Varno as he struggled under the quivering folds of the reassembled kite he had insisted on carrying from the cabin despite the heavy wind.

Mayor Van Gribin approached, flanked by the four council members. He raised his voice so that all could hear. "My-y-y-y son-n-n! This is a historic date that the people of Kalvala will never forget. I need not tell you that all our best wishes are with you in this valiant effort to free us from our winter travail. The entire council joins me in—"

"Tulo!" his uncle roared. "Hurry, please! I cannot hold this red monster any longer. It wants to fly, and if I am not careful it will take me with it. Please, let us do whatever we must to put it in the air . . . quickly, quickly!"

Varno raised the kite high above his head and waited anxiously. Finally the star tree bent under a powerful blast of wind and Tulo screamed,

"Now!" Varno heaved the kite skyward with the roar of a weight lifter, and instantly it leaped aloft as if fired from a catapult.

Tulo needed all his strength to control the line as it snarled and whined through his fingers. Soon he could feel warmth from the rope's friction tearing against his leather gloves. He raised his head just in time to see the kite's white tails disappear into the shifting ceiling of snow-filled clouds.

More than three agonizing hours passed. The villagers were becoming restless. Perspiration covered Tulo's face despite the cold, and the inside of his mouth felt and tasted like dried reindeer meat. Sharp stabbing pains ripped across his shoulders, and his right knee was numb. His head throbbed and his eyes ached from the wind. He wanted to quit, to let go, to end the agony . . . but he couldn't. He owed this flight to Acabar . . . and Mama . . . and the village.

Then, just as on that first flight, the upward pull on his line suddenly stopped.

"What is it, Tulo? Have we caught something?"

"I don't know, Jaana," he panted. "I hope so. Stay by my side while I try to take in the line."

Tulo tugged and the line offered no resistance. Gently he applied downward pressure, hand over hand, and the rope dutifully fell until the ground beneath his feet was covered with twine. The noisy villagers pressed closer.

"I see it, I see it!" a woman's voice shrieked from the crowd.

"I see it, too," screamed Jaana. "A light . . . a light . . . and it's coming closer. Tulo, we've done it, we've done it! We have another star!"

The crowd surged forward, pushing and shoving, crying and laughing, as they fought to congratulate and touch their young hero.

"Stand back," Varno yelled as he raised his hands to protect his nephew. "Please, please, give him room . . . and be careful! That thing could kill you if it fell on you. Back away, please, I beg you!"

With each tug of the rope the star descended, floating silently and regally through the darkness, bathing each uplifted face in an aura of soft orange light. Varno, with rare tears streaming down his leathery face, watched admiringly as Tulo expertly guided his kite and the small star until they were directly above the star tree. At last the young man carefully eased his luminescent captive down until it came to rest on the same strong limbs that had embraced Acabar.

Long after the celebration ended in the meadow and Jaana was in bed, Tulo, too excited to sleep, returned to the meadow. He climbed through the tree's branches until he was within reach of the star. This one was smaller than Acabar, and its light was a constantly shifting series of pink and yellow hues. Tulo's hand was trembling as he reached forward until his fingers were gently rubbing against the warm hard surface.

"How beautiful you are," he sighed. "Thank you for answering my prayers."

"You're very welcome."

Tulo caught hold of the nearest bough or he would have fallen to the ground. "Another talking star? It cannot be."

"Young man, we all can talk. Have you already forgotten what Acabar told you? I'm sorry if I startled you. I would have thought you'd be quite accustomed to conversing with stars by now."

"You know about . . . Star Acabar?"

"Yes, I do."

"Star Acabar is dead," Tulo whispered. "See his . . . his body, under the tree."

"He never should have come here! We all warned him that this mission was far more dangerous than the one he completed so perfectly over Bethlehem, but he wasn't worried in the least. He had great faith that you would help him to return to the heavens after he accomplished what he came to do. As your guiding star he's been tracking you ever since you were born. Many of us have at least one human we watch over and try to help without being too obvious. Mine is an adorable little girl in a place you call Rhodesia. Acabar, as he watched you make great progress with your writing, became convinced that you were something very special. Then you had that unfortunate accident and stopped believing in yourself. He was so upset. Only time I ever saw him that way. He tried, time and again, to get through to you but your mind was so filled with defeat and self-pity that it was impossible, even for him. Finally he decided that his only hope of saving you from yourself was to come down here."

Tulo lowered his head. "Star Acabar gave his precious life for me—a nobody from a village so tiny that hardly anyone knows or cares we are here."

"My dear boy, how wrong you are! God has never created a 'nobody'! And no village is so small that it is unknown or unloved by its Creator.

Furthermore, you must grieve no more for your friend Acabar. He is not dead!"

"Oh, yes, he is! See? Down there . . . his cinder . . . under the tree."

"I repeat, Acabar is not dead. That cinder may have been his, but just as you will leave your body when you are called to the Kingdom of Forever, so has Acabar. He's back up there, somewhere . . . watching and listening to us even now, I'm certain. Of course he must begin his life and career anew, but in fifty thousand years or so he'll be flying around again, just as before. It won't be very long."

Tulo's wide eyes joyfully swept the star-filled sky. "That is the most wonderful news I have ever heard! Star Acabar is alive! Star Acabar is alive! Oh, how I wish I could see him again!"

"You will, young man, you will."

"Thank you for bringing me such good news, uh—uh . . ."

"I am called Lirra."

"Lirra? Your voice—it's different from Star Acabar's—as if you were a . . . a . . ."

"A woman? I am. I am a woman."

"Really?"

"Why not?" asked the star. "What makes you think that all heavenly beings are male any more than earth people?"

"Lirra is a pretty name. You are very pretty."

The star glowed a deep scarlet. "Thank you, Tulo. A sincere compliment is an excellent way to begin a friendship."

The youth was silent for several moments. Then he asked, haltingly, "Star Lirra, if Star Acabar risked so much to come here to help me . . . why

89

are you here? Was it not just as dangerous for you to come?"

There was no reply.

Tulo bravely persisted. "Star Lirra, why did you come? Why did you let me catch you in my kite?"

The star's light increased in intensity. "I had to come. Acabar and I were very close for a long time. His greatest ambition was to see this small planet, that he loved so much, achieve its full potential. In the beginning I did not share his dream. Time after time I would point out all the horrible deeds that earth people commit every day, through their misuse of the power of choice. He would reply by telling me of your great heroes and philosophers and saints and prophets and writers and inventors. Then he would take me on flights around this planet and show me billions of earth people who needed guidance and hope as they struggled to make a better life for themselves and their children. He convinced me. And according to Acabar, you, Tulo Mattis, are destined to be a great star of hope for all humanity."

"A star of hope? My mother once said that about me—and my writing. But I don't know how that will ever be possible, Star Lirra. I was part of a herd going nowhere, like our reindeer, until Star Acabar came. He taught me about myself—and life—but all my dreams died when he fell to the ground."

Lirra abruptly changed the subject before the youth could continue his self-pity. "Young man, what are you planning to do with me? I assume you're not going to leave me here, in this lovely tree, shedding my light on this meadow."

Tulo rubbed his forehead and sighed. "Star Lirra, I don't know what to do. I wanted to catch another star to help our poor village, but after listening to everyone's advice I am very confused. The one thing I do know is that I will not allow them to move you from place to place. Wherever it is decided that you are to go, there you will remain until the sun returns. Then my kite will take you back to the sky as I had planned to do with Star Acabar."

Lirra sighed. "I'll go wherever you wish, but if the choice were mine I would select the schoolhouse. I love the little people because every child born is a new message from God. It's probably my woman's heart speaking, instead of my mind, but I would be most pleased to illuminate a classroom for Kalvala's girls and boys."

Tulo smiled sadly. "Soon I shall lose you too."

"Young man, listen well! Nothing is ever lost. Someday when you are once again with your mama and papa and Acabar and me you will understand. Even Acabar's gift for you is not lost. You asked why I came here. Tulo, I came here to honor Acabar by helping him to fulfill his dreams for this world —and you. I came to bring you his gift!"

"Credenda? *You* have Credenda?"

"I assisted Acabar in the collection of all the wisdom that he eventually condensed into his simple but beautiful work. I know Credenda by heart. When I saw what happened here last week, I had to come when you flew your kite again."

"Then there is still a chance for me! Star Lirra, what can I say? Thank you for coming, oh, thank you!"

"Hold on, Tulo. There is one other matter of supreme importance that we must discuss. Acabar believed that one courageous human, armed with faith, knowledge, and truth, could change this world. It has been done before. He wanted *you* to have Credenda—but remember that he also wanted you to do everything in your power to share his gift with others. Tell me. How do you plan to notify the people of the world of your legacy so that they can take its words to their hearts?"

Tulo closed his eyes and pondered the star's monumental question. He murmured, "Words . . . words bound in leather . . . your destiny is beyond Kalvala. . . . Star of hope . . . look up . . . reach out. . . ."

"What's that? What are you saying?" Lirra asked.

"I will find a way, Star Lirra, I promise you. I *will* find a way."

"Very well. I leave it all in your hands. Return here tomorrow with your green ledger and I shall deliver Credenda to you, word for word. Then you can notify your schoolmaster that he is to have a guest until the sun returns. And if he cannot use me, I'll go wherever you wish. Good night, little friend."

Early on the following morning Tulo dressed and hurried to the meadow. In less than an hour Acabar's gift was passed from its heavenly messenger to its earthly courier.

Sixteen

CREDENDA

Turn away from the crowd & its fruitless pursuit of fame & gold. Never look back as you close your door to the sorry tumult of greed & ambition. Wipe away your tears of failure & misfortune. Lay aside your heavy load & rest until your heart is still. Be at peace. Already it is later than you think, for your earthly life, at best, is only the blink of an eye between two eternities. Be unafraid. Nothing here can harm you except yourself. Do that which you dread & cherish those victories with pride. Concentrate your energy. To be everywhere is to be nowhere. Be jealous of your time, since it is your greatest treasure. Reconsider your goals. Before you set your heart too much on anything, examine how happy they are who already possess what you desire. Love your family & count your blessings. Reflect on how eagerly they would be sought if you did not have them. Put aside your impossible dreams & complete the task at hand no matter how distasteful. All great achievements come from working and waiting. Be patient. God's delays are never God's denials. Hold on. Hold fast. Know that your paymaster is always near. What you sow, good or evil, that you will reap. Never blame your condition on others. You are what you are through your choice alone. Learn to live with honest poverty, if you must, & turn to more important matters than transporting gold to your grave. Never meet trouble halfway. Anxiety is the rust of life; when you add tomorrow's burdens to today's their weight becomes unbearable. Avoid the mourner's bench & give thanks, instead, for your defeats. You would not receive them if you did not need them. Always learn from others. He who teaches himself has a fool for a master. Be careful. Do not overload your conscience. Conduct your life as if it were spent in an arena filled with tattlers. Avoid boasting. If you see anything in you that puffs you with pride look closer & you will find more than enough to make you humble. Be wise. Realize that all men are not created equal, for there is no equality in nature, yet no man was ever born whose work was not born with him. Work every day as if it were your first, yet tenderly treat the lives you touch as if they will all end at midnight. Love everyone, even those who deny you, for hate is a luxury you cannot afford. Seek out those in need. Learn that he who delivers with one hand will always gather with two. Be of good cheer. Above all, remember that very little is needed to make a happy life. Look up. Reach out. Cling simply to God & journey quietly on your pathway to forever with charity & a smile. When you depart it will be said by all that your legacy was a better world than the one you found.

Seventeen

☆

Jaana seized the rein from her brother's open hand and pulled with all her strength until the sledge came to a halt.

"Tulo, what is wrong with you?"

"N-nothing. Why?"

"I thought we were going to the schoolhouse to tell Mr. Nobis that we are giving him our star."

"We are."

"Tulo!" she exclaimed with an exasperated shake of her head. "We have already passed the schoolhouse. Are you ill? You haven't spoken since we left home."

"I'm sorry, Jaana," her brother replied in a strange and unfamiliar monotone. "I've been thinking about many things. Someday you will understand."

Tulo retrieved the rein from his sister and turned their old animal back in the direction they had come. Several barking dogs escorted their sledge as it noisily plowed through the morning blackness to the rhythmic clank of Kala's neck bell.

They found Arrol Nobis reading in his empty classroom. Immediately Jaana blurted, "Sir, we are giving you our new star for the school!"

The young schoolmaster's head jerked as if he had been struck. When he recovered he rose and embraced both his pupils. "Thank you, both. Your kind offer touches me deeply. It is because of people like you that Kalvala is a beautiful place despite its barren lands and terrible climate."

The schoolmaster returned to his chair and lowered his head. His voice was muffled.

"We are rich only through what we give and poor only through what we keep. I have been deeply ashamed of myself ever since I came to your cabin and offered to help you enter the university, Tulo, in exchange for your star. I should have been helping you all along—with love. Instead I selfishly placed a price on my friendship and tried to force you to ransom your future with the most precious thing you now possess."

Tulo and Jaana had never seen their schoolmaster in this condition. Tulo touched his arm gently and said, "Sir, we gave no thought to your helping me with the university. We just want you to have our star for the children. The university is not very important to me any more."

Arrol Nobis drew Tulo close and they embraced again. Then the schoolmaster held his prize pupil at arm's length and stared into his eyes. "Your face feels very warm . . . and your eyes are streaked with blood. Tulo, are you all right?"

"Yes, I'm just very tired. Will you take our star, sir?"

The schoolmaster smiled but shook his head firmly. "No, but I will help you with the university whenever you are ready. As to your star, I suggest you give your beautiful light to the church. There is no other rightful place for it in all of Kalvala. It was God's hand that directed your kite to the first star—and the second. What belongs to God must be returned to God.

"My pupils will survive as children always do, and we shall all work extra hours when the sun returns. Boys and girls can adjust to anything but the loss of love, and there certainly will never be a shortage of that among our people."

When the children were seated in their sledge Tulo turned to their teacher as he stood in the schoolhouse doorway. "What belongs to God must be returned to God!"

The schoolmaster nodded and waved good-bye.

Pastor Bjork was sitting alone in the front pew of his church. One small candle shone from the altar.

"My dear children, how good it is to see you. I've been in here so long, praying to God for my forgiveness, that I'm afraid I've lost all sense of time."

Jaana was puzzled. "Forgiveness—for you?"

"Oh, yes," the prelate replied sadly. "I allowed my own petty self-interests to blind me to everything that I have preached and lived all my life. After I dispensed nearly all my candles and fuel to the needy, as God would expect me to do, I then lost faith that our church could survive in this brief moment of darkness when it has survived the threat of darkness for centuries. I came begging for your star when so many need it far more than I do. What a terrible and selfish person I have become in my old age. Oh, Lord, deliver me from that evil man, myself."

Two trembling children backed slowly out of the church before Pastor Bjork remembered to ask them why they had come.

Dr. Malni also refused their star. Only this morning, he told them, the mayor had given him a small supply of oil which would keep his lamps and stove burning for at least another week at the clinic. He thanked the children warmly and promised that he would never forget their generous offer. He also said that although he had little compassion for LaVeeg and his methods, there was much to be said about the importance of the store to the village.

"Mr. LaVeeg," announced Tulo, when they eventually stood before the store owner at his cash register, "we have decided to let you have our star for your store. You may keep it here until the sun returns."

LaVeeg began to giggle with joy until a coughing spell nearly bent him double. When he recovered he came from behind the counter and patted both children on their cheeks. "How wise of you two! How very wise! And profitable too, I might add. I'll keep my bargain with you. Trust me, trust me. You will never regret this decision."

"Sir." Jaana jumped up and down to catch the old man's attention. "Tulo and I do not want any of your money. We are only loaning you the star so that the people of the village will not have to shop in darkness."

The store owner's smile vanished, and he glared at Jaana until she moved closer to her brother. "What's that you say? No money? You want nothing for the star? I don't understand. Why, why?"

Tulo lowered his eyes and said, "We . . . we wanted to give the star to the schoolhouse."

"That would have been silly," LaVeeg snapped. "Nobis couldn't pay you anything. Nothing!"

"We didn't want anything. Mr. Nobis thanked us but told us to give it to Pastor Bjork for his church, and Pastor Bjork was sorry he had ever asked for the star, so we went to the clinic."

"And Malni refused it, too?" cried the stunned merchant. "Is that why you're here?"

"Y-y-yes."

LaVeeg leaned across the counter. "What's wrong with the star? What are you two keeping from me?"

"Nothing. It's a beautiful star."

"Hmmm, I don't know, I don't know. I want that star very much. But why has everyone refused it? Bjork and Nobis and the doctor, they're not very smart but they're not fools either. I certainly don't want any more problems around here. For all I know the stupid thing might explode—or burn this place down. Anything could happen! After all, what do we know about stars?"

"Not as much as they know about us."

"What's that, young man? What's that you say?"

Tulo stared at the ceiling and remained silent.

LaVeeg pounded on the counter in frustration until the drawer of his ancient cash register sprang open. He slammed it shut and yelled, "I just can't afford to take the chance. I could lose my entire life's assets with that thing. I could be ruined! I've changed my mind. I don't want your star. Now go! You two have caused enough trouble!"

Tulo and Jaana sang all the way back to their cabin. Before they went to bed they sat at their table with hot glowcake and coffee and decided, after great deliberation, that it would still not be fair to move the star into their cabin.

Instead, for the next seven weeks, they shared their lustrous visitor with everyone in Kalvala. As soon as the storm ended children came to the meadow to play. Arrol Nobis conducted classes near the tree where it was warm. Pastor Bjork held his Sunday services there, and even LaVeeg parked his sledge close by, filled with canned goods and other supplies.

And then . . . one day . . . the vagrant sun raised a small arc of its golden circle above the horizon, and Tulo knew the time had come to fulfill his pact with Star Lirra.

To return her to the sky would not be difficult on the arms of his strong red kite.

To share Credenda with the entire world was another matter. Still, after living under the spell of its words each day for seven weeks, he knew there was only one way he could be certain of success.

First, he must alert the people of Kalvala to the

100

priceless treasure that had been delivered to them, through him.

They—in their own way, and in their own time —would eventually present the gift of Acabar to the world.

Eighteen

☆

As it had been on that memorable day when Lirra came down to earth, the meadow was once again filled with village families as the hour of the star's departure drew near. This time, however, they clustered together in silent, unsmiling groups as if they were outside their church before a funeral.

Tulo, his eyes clouded, lethargically rolled several meters of twine and rope into a coil and inched his way up through the branches of the star tree until he was close to Lirra.

"Come now, young man," she whispered consolingly, "there's no reason to look so sad. We'll see each other again."

"I know," he whispered.

"Tulo, you sound and look very strange, as if you were in a trance of some sort. Are you confident that you can handle this launching? Are you well?"

"I'm fine, Star Lirra. Please don't worry."

"Well then, smile. Stop acting as if your world was about to end."

Tulo nodded.

He had tied several more knots in the line he had wrapped around the star's exterior before Lirra asked, "Have you given any more thought as to how you plan to bring Credenda to the world's attention?"

"Trust me, Star Lirra, trust me. I have a plan."

"I do trust you, little man, more than ever after these weeks we have spent together. I came here to teach you. Instead I have learned a great deal from you . . . and from observing the others. Acabar was correct. All that earth people need is a light to guide them: a star of hope, as your mother said in her prophecy to you. Well, farewell for now. I love you, little man."

"I love you too, Star Lirra."

Tulo tossed the four separate lines he had tied around the glowing sphere down to his uncle, who attached each to the spine of the kite. Then he silently caressed the star once more and climbed down through the branches to the ground.

The youth waited until the last piece of rope was attached firmly to the kite before he asked, "Uncle Varno, if anything ever happened to me would you take care of Jaana?"

Varno turned to his nephew with a look of bewilderment. "Of course. Your aunt and I have always wanted you two to come live with us so that we could watch over both of you. Why do you ask such a question at a time like this?"

"I was just wondering."

"Well, stop wondering about such things and let's get down to our business while you still have this strong wind."

Tulo limped toward Jaana, who was busily unwinding twine from the large ball. He reached down, removed both her hands from the rope, and brought them close to his chest. "Jaana, do you know where I keep the green ledger?"

"Yes. It's in the big drawer of your dresser. Why?"

"Will you promise that if anything ever happens to me you will give the ledger to Mr. Nobis? He will know what to do with it."

"Yes, but . . ."

Tulo smiled and kissed her on her nose. Then he hurried back to the big tree, which was now bending from warm westerly winds. He reached for the line and pulled several meters through his hands so that Varno would have sufficient slack to toss the kite skyward. As he slid the rope through his fingers, he noticed a weak section where several strands had separated. Tulo removed his hunting knife, made two cuts, dropped the damaged rope to the ground, and knotted the healthy pieces together. Now he was ready.

At a nod from his nephew, Varno raised the kite above his head while making certain that the lines which led from the star to the kite were free of all branches. He waited, struggling with all his strength to hold the kite. Then Tulo nodded again and Varno flung the giant kite away from him. The sound of the wind colliding against the red cloth was as loud as a rifle shot, and as the crowd moaned Varno quickly turned his head toward the tree to watch the star. The four ropes attached to the silver globe tightened. The kite jerked convulsively as it tugged against the star. At last the star was free, swaying in short pendulum arcs of pink and silver as it moved higher, pursuing the red kite up . . . up . . . into the dark blue twilight.

All eyes were on the star except one pair.

Tulo reached down and removed his knife again. Swiftly and tightly he wound the rope leading up to the climbing kite around his wrist several times. Then, with a single slashing motion, he cut the rope below his wrist away from the large unwinding ball of twine on the ground.

Jaana screamed first. "Tulo, Tulo, my beautiful brother!" She raced to her uncle and pounded on his chest frantically. "Uncle Varno, stop him! Save him! Do something! Please!"

Varno pressed Jaana close to his chest and watched with helpless horror as his young nephew soared skyward, trailing beneath his beloved star and his kite.

Soon even the shining ball had disappeared from sight in the gathering dusk, and all that remained visible to the awestruck people of Kalvala were the first bright stars of an early spring evening.

Nineteen

☆

More than two months passed before Arrol Nobis could bring himself to open and read the green ledger which a grief-stricken Jaana had delivered to him shortly after Tulo's ascent.

The awesome significance behind each entry, childishly scrawled on page after page of ledger paper, was a greater burden than the young schoolmaster could bear alone. He asked that the mayor call an emergency meeting of the village council, and the members listened in stunned silence as he read the entire diary to them, including Credenda.

LaVeeg, as usual, was the first to speak. "Tourists! If this matter is handled and promoted properly our village will become the greatest attraction in all of Finland—in all of Europe! The museum at Inari, the gold panning near Karigasniemi, the salmon fishing on the Tana, old Vardöhus Castle: all of these will become insignificant compared with a visit to Kalvala. Many hotels and stores, even an airport, will be built to handle the thousands, the hundreds of thousands, who will journey from every part of the world in order to touch the cinder and rub the tree and visit the cabin where young Tulo lived. And money—they will have money in their purses. The souvenir concession alone will be worth millions!"

Pastor Bjork exclaimed, "We shall have a shrine in the meadow as great as Lourdes!"

"Our village will grow until it becomes the largest city north of the capital!" Mayor Van Gribin exulted.

Even Arrol Nobis smiled. "And our new school will be the finest in the entire province."

It was the mayor who finally called a halt to their daydreams. He reminded the council that no one outside of Kalvala was even aware of the strange and wonderful events that had taken place in their village. He warned them that none of their grand hopes would ever materialize unless they decided on a plan that would effectively proclaim Kalvala's miracle to the people of the entire world.

Pastor Bjork agreed. "After all, is that not why Tulo gave his precious life? Kindly forgive my religious analogy, but was not our young lad's great sacrifice intended to awaken our people, and eventually the world, to the great truths of love and compassion contained in Acabar's gift? Did not that babe born in Bethlehem, under Acabar's own bright light, also offer his earthly body, long ago, to help us realize that the kingdom of God truly is as close to each of us as our hearts?"

After long hours of discussion it was finally decided that Arrol Nobis would be granted a leave of absence and would depart immediately, at the expense of the village, for Helsinki, where he would tell the story of the miracle of Kalvala to the leading newspapers, magazines, and radio stations. LaVeeg suggested that perhaps Kalvala should be renamed, appropriately, before the world's journalists began arriving to do their feature stories, but this motion, although accepted unanimously, was tabled until Van Gribin could check on the necessary legal requirements for such a change.

Three weeks later, Arrol Nobis returned from the nation's capital a beaten man. Two editors from Finland's largest newspaper, the *Sanomat*, after patiently listening to his story and taking many notes, laughingly accused the young schoolmaster of wasting their time with a fraud so amateurish that not even the most gullible would be fooled. The green ledger was casually dismissed as no more than contrived fiction and fantasy. A star coming down to earth indeed! A talking star? The young teacher must suffer from hallucinations— or worse.

A reporter from the *Uusi Suomi* told the schoolmaster it was the most ingenious plan he had ever heard to attract tourists and land buyers to the barren tundra country, and he asked Arrol to convey, to the village fathers of Kalvala, his utmost admiration for concocting such a scheme. But certainly he could not jeopardize the integrity of his paper by becoming an accomplice to such an outlandish hoax.

One radio station commentator did indicate some willingness to promote the village, the cinder, and the star tree—for a price, of course. Arrol was even invited to be his guest on several programs to read from Tulo's green ledger in exchange for an equitable share of the profits from what the radio personality was certain would become an extremely lucrative real-estate operation.

No one believed any part of Arrol's story, nor would they accept the words in the green ledger as any more than just another Lapp fairy tale.

The mayor and his council listened to Arrol's report with shocked stillness. When he was finished there was no immediate response to the mayor's request for comments on so tragic a turn of events.

Finally Pastor Bjork rose, cleared his throat, and said, "Gentlemen, what is to be will be. Apparently God has no plans for Kalvala, or its people, to become further involved in this matter. Perhaps the time is not right. Still I have supreme faith that someday, in a manner we cannot even conceive in this present hour of disappointment, Tulo's wish will come true and the words contained in the Credenda will become an eternal monument to his bravery and his love. Yet no one can deny that our people remain in great debt to him. Therefore I propose that we place a memorial stone with an appropriate bronze tablet under the big tree, close by the fallen star, to perpetually honor this outstanding young man. I also suggest that such a monument be purchased by the people of Kalvala."

The pastor's motions were quickly seconded and the mayor offered to contact his friends in Göteborg, who were expert in the art of fine castings, as soon as a decision was made as to the inscription which would be placed on the tablet. Arrol Nobis was delegated to select words that would be most meaningful, and his choice, easily made, was unanimously approved at the following meeting.

On the first anniversary of Tulo's departure the

meadow was once again filled with nearly every man, woman, and child of Kalvala. Both the mayor and the pastor spoke briefly before Varno slowly led his small niece under the big tree close to the monument, which had been covered by a purple velvet altar cloth borrowed from the church. She glanced up at her uncle with frightened eyes until he nodded sympathetically, gesturing toward the cloth.

Jaana stepped forward, clutched a corner of velvet, and pulled, exposing a slender square piece of granite not half her size. The crowd moved closer as she knelt before the tablet and silently read, below her brother's name, words that had been written to console another sister's loss, nearly two thousand years ago:

TULO MATTIS
1947–1961

DO NOT GRUDGE YOUR BROTHER HIS REST. HE HAS AT LAST BECOME FREE, SAFE AND IM- MORTAL, AND RANGES JOYOUS THROUGH THE BOUNDLESS HEAVENS; HE HAS LEFT THIS LOW- LYING REGION AND HAS SOARED UPWARDS TO THAT PLACE WHICH RECEIVES IN ITS HAPPY BOSOM THE SOULS SET FREE FROM THE CHAINS OF MATTER.

YOUR BROTHER HAS NOT LOST THE LIGHT OF DAY, BUT HAS OBTAINED A MORE ENDURING LIGHT. HE HAS NOT LEFT US, BUT HAS GONE ON BEFORE.

—SENECA

The green ledger gathered dust on the top shelf of the living room closet in the Nobis home for several years, until one day, Arrol's wife, Kirsti, suggested that perhaps he should return it to Jaana, who was soon to marry Teno Van Gribin, as part of their wedding present.

Jaana received the green ledger with mixed emotions. Although she had never forgotten its existence, she had no desire to reopen her own wounds of anguish over the loss of her brother. She packed the diary in a trunk without opening it, and after her marriage the trunk was one of four that accompanied the young couple to Helsinki, where Teno had accepted a position with a law firm following his graduation from the university. Jaana sold the cabin and land, including the meadow, to her father-in-law, who immediately donated the meadow to the village. Before long it became known as Star Tree Park.

A daughter was born to Jaana and Teno during their second year in the capital. She was christened Inga, after her grandmother. As children always do, she brought good fortune to her parents. Teno was recruited for the position of assistant counsel on the Finnish staff of the United Nations. Four years later, because of his excellent record, he was promoted to serve on the staff attached to the General Assembly committee dealing with social, humanitarian, and cultural problems. The young family moved to New York City and rented a small apartment, with balcony, on the East River, near the United Nations building. The green ledger was once again unpacked and placed on a closet shelf.

One warm spring evening, as Jaana and Teno were relaxing on the balcony, watching the lights from scores of boats ripple softly on the dark water, Inga climbed on her mother's lap, looked up at the stars, and asked, "Mama, will you tell me the story of Uncle Tulo and the stars again, please?"

Jaana shook her head and glanced helplessly at her husband, who puffed contentedly on his pipe and pretended not to hear.

"Inga, you have heard the story a hundred times. By now you know it as well as I do."

The small blond head snuggled deeper into her mother's arms. "It does not matter. Please tell me again."

By the time Jaana was describing the second star's visit to Kalvala, her child's eyes were closed. "She's asleep, Teno."

"I'm not," piped a voice from her chest. Then a small hand came close to Jaana's face, one finger pointing up into the sky. "Look, Mama, look, Daddy! It's Tulo's kite! I see Tulo's kite!"

Jaana paled and sat upright, squinting to follow the line of her young daughter's finger. Teno, whose one regret had been leaving his telescope behind when they packed, broke into a gale of laughter as he realized what had caught Inga's attention. He left his chair and sat on the balcony floor next to the child, reaching up at the same time to take hold of his wife's hand, which was unusually cold. "No, darling. That's not Tulo's kite. Those seven stars are called the Big Dipper. See how it is shaped, with a handle of three stars and the square dipper of four? Do you see it?"

"It's not a dipper, Daddy, it's not! It's Tulo's kite, isn't it, Mama?"

Jaana's voice was only a whisper. "I don't know, darling, I don't know."

"It *is* Tulo's kite. Look! The four stars are the corners of the kite and the three behind are the tail. See, Daddy?"

Teno looked past his small daughter at Jaana, who nodded weakly. "Yes, dear, now I see. You're right, it is his kite."

Suddenly the child raised her hand once more. "Now I see Tulo, I see Tulo!"

Jaana raised both hands to her mouth and cried, "Inga, please. That's enough!"

"But I do, Mama, I do see Tulo! Look! See the middle star of the three in the tail?"

"Yes."

"There's another tiny star close to the middle star. See it? It's Tulo! It's Tulo still riding his kite!"

Jaana strained her tear-filled eyes, focusing intently on the middle star of the tail. Finally she exclaimed, "My God, Teno, there *is* another small star there. Look!"

Her husband put his hand firmly on her shoulder. His voice broke as he replied. "I don't have to look, Jaana. There are three stars in the handle—or the tail, as Inga calls it—and their Arabic names, in astronomy, are Alkaid, Mizar, and Alioth. Close to the middle star, Mizar, is a smaller star quite difficult to see with the naked eye. That star is called Alcor. Jaana, do you have any idea what Alcor means in Arabic? I'll tell you. It means 'the rider.' "

Inga became frightened by her mother's sobs, and with her two small hands she desperately wiped the moisture from Jaana's soft cheeks. "Don't cry, Mama. You must not be sad. This is the happiest day of our lives. Tonight we found Tulo, and as long as we live he'll always be up there to watch over us."

If you look, you too will discover Tulo, with your eyes . . . and your heart . . . and thus the words in the green ledger will be fulfilled. . . . For now its secrets are a part of you . . . and they will be with you always . . . even unto the Kingdom of Forever.

THE END

ABOUT THE AUTHORS

OG MANDINO'S nine books, with multi-million copy sales, make him, without doubt, the most widely read inspirational and self-help author in the world during the past decade.

In 1976, at the age of fifty-two, he shocked the publishing industry by resigning his presidency of SUCCESS UNLIMITED magazine to devote all his time to writing and lecturing and he is now one of the most sought-after speakers in the country.

Countless thousands in seventeen nations, from American corporate executives to Japanese factory workers, from Mexican prison convicts to Dutch housewives, from National Football League coaches to nuns in the Philippines, have acknowledged, in their letters, the great debt they owe Og Mandino for the miracle his words have wrought in their lives.

BUDDY KAYE is best known as a gifted lyricist whose songs have exceeded 50 million record sales around the world. Highly motivated and achievement-oriented, Kaye has excelled in every field of endeavor that he has undertaken: musician, lyricist, teacher, lecturer, and record producer of his Grammy Award-winning LP "The Little Prince," narrated by Richard Burton. *The Gift of Acabar* is his first published novel.

Another inspirational masterpiece
by the author of
The Greatest Salesman in the World

THE GREATEST
SUCCESS
IN THE WORLD
By Og Mandino

A BANTAM HARDCOVER

At last, after six years, comes the stirring companion
volume to *THE GREATEST SALESMAN IN THE
WORLD, THE GREATEST SECRET IN THE
WORLD* and *THE GREATEST MIRACLE IN THE
WORLD*. In his unique storytelling style, Og Mandino
transports you back to Jericho during the time of
Christ, where you will meet a most unlikely hero with
a priceless legacy—THE COMMANDMENTS OF
SUCCESS. By using these commandments wisely, you
can end your old life and start a new life filled with
love, pride, peace of mind and happiness.

"Anyone who wants true success would do well to read
this masterpiece."

—Norman Vincent Peale

*Read THE GREATEST SUCCESS IN THE WORLD,
on sale September 15, 1981 wherever Bantam hard-
covers are sold.*

Heartwarming Books
of
Faith and Inspiration